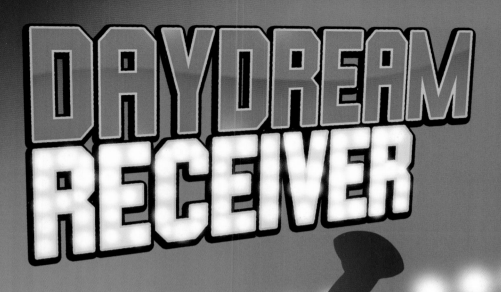

DAYDREAM RECEIVER

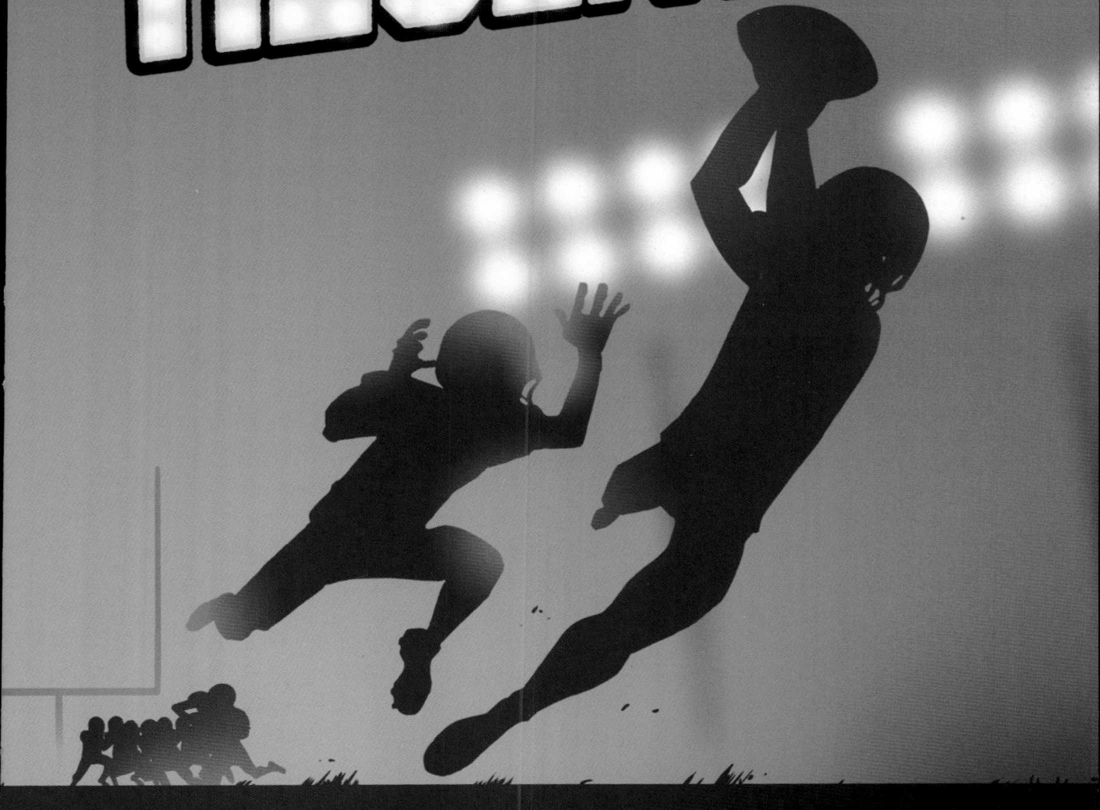

STONE ARCH BOOKS

JAKE MADDOX
GRAPHIC NOVELS

Jake Maddox Graphic Novels are published by
Stone Arch Books, a Capstone imprint
1710 Roe Crest Drive
North Mankato, Minnesota 56003

www.mycapstone.com

Library of Congress Cataloging-in-Publication Data is available on the Library of Congress website.

ISBN: 978-1-4965-3702-7 (library binding)
ISBN: 978-1-4965-3706-5 (paperback)
ISBN: 978-1-4965-3722-5 (ebook PDF)

Summary: Gus Blackburn is a dreamer. He dreams of catching the winning touchdown in the big game. He dreams of being as popular as the team quarterback, and of smooth talking with the girls in his school. But in reality Gus is an oversized, third-string receiver who rides the pine more than running routes on the field. However, with the homecoming game fast approaching, Gus is determined to show his teammates that his size won't keep him from living out his dreams.

Editor: Aaron Sautter
Designer: Brann Garvey
Production: Gene Bentdahl

Printed in the United States of America.
082018 000044

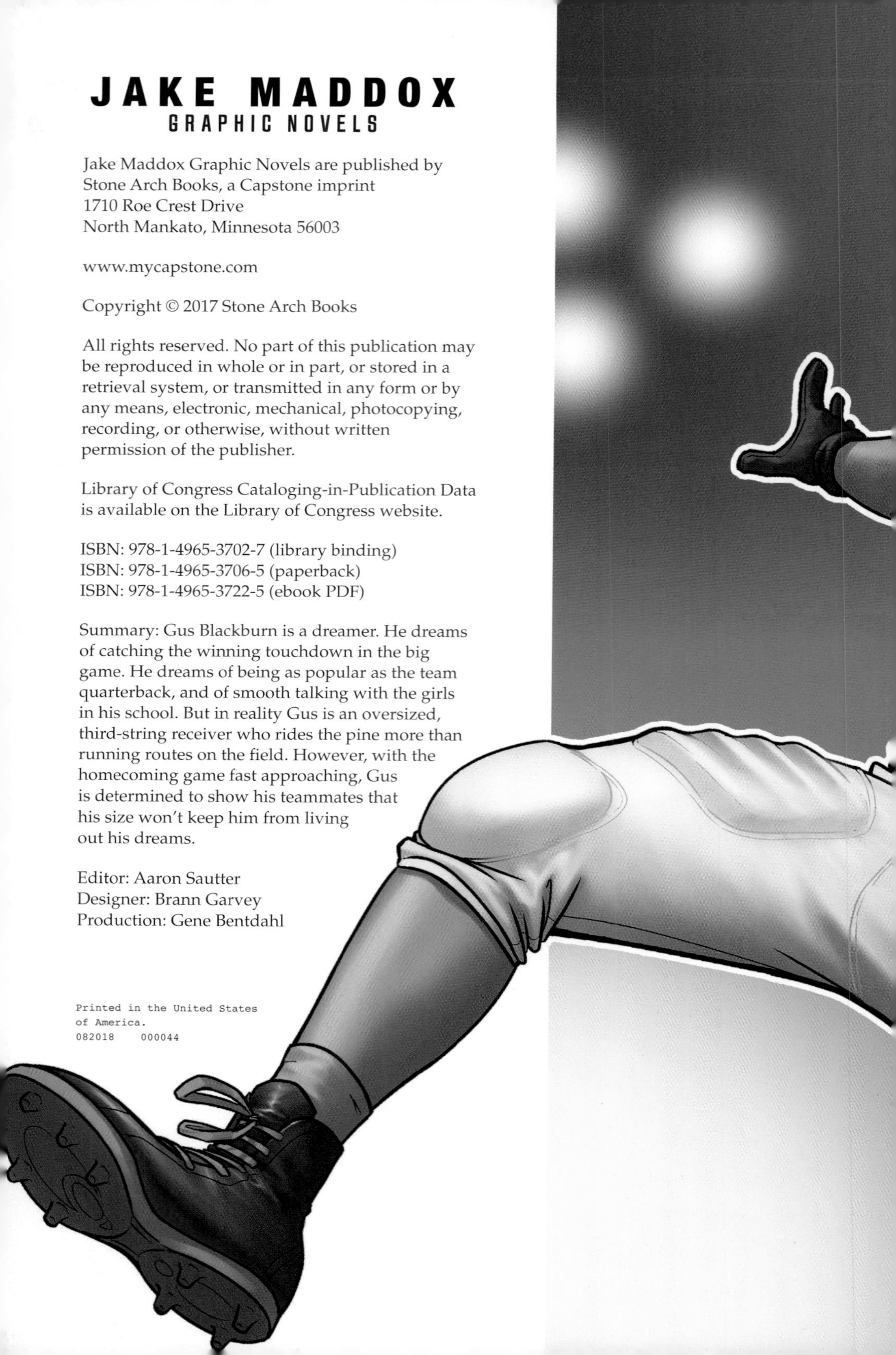

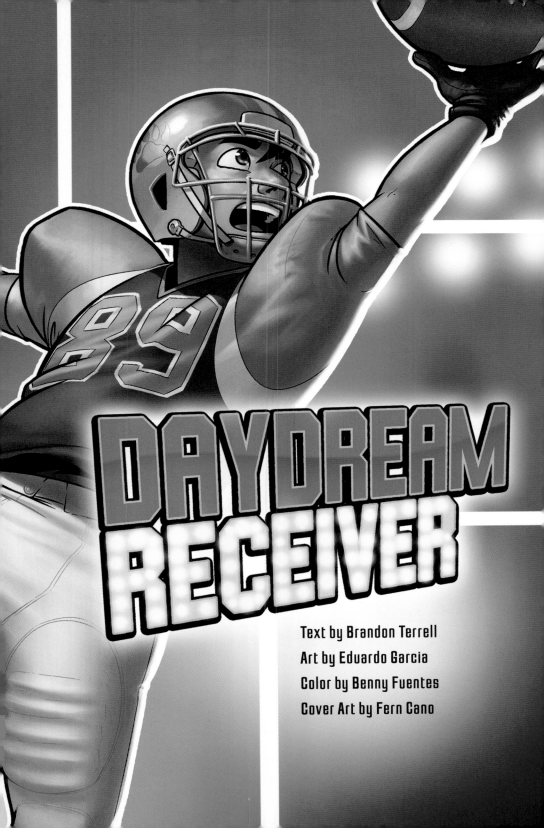

DAYDREAM RECEIVER

Text by Brandon Terrell

Art by Eduardo Garcia

Color by Benny Fuentes

Cover Art by Fern Cano

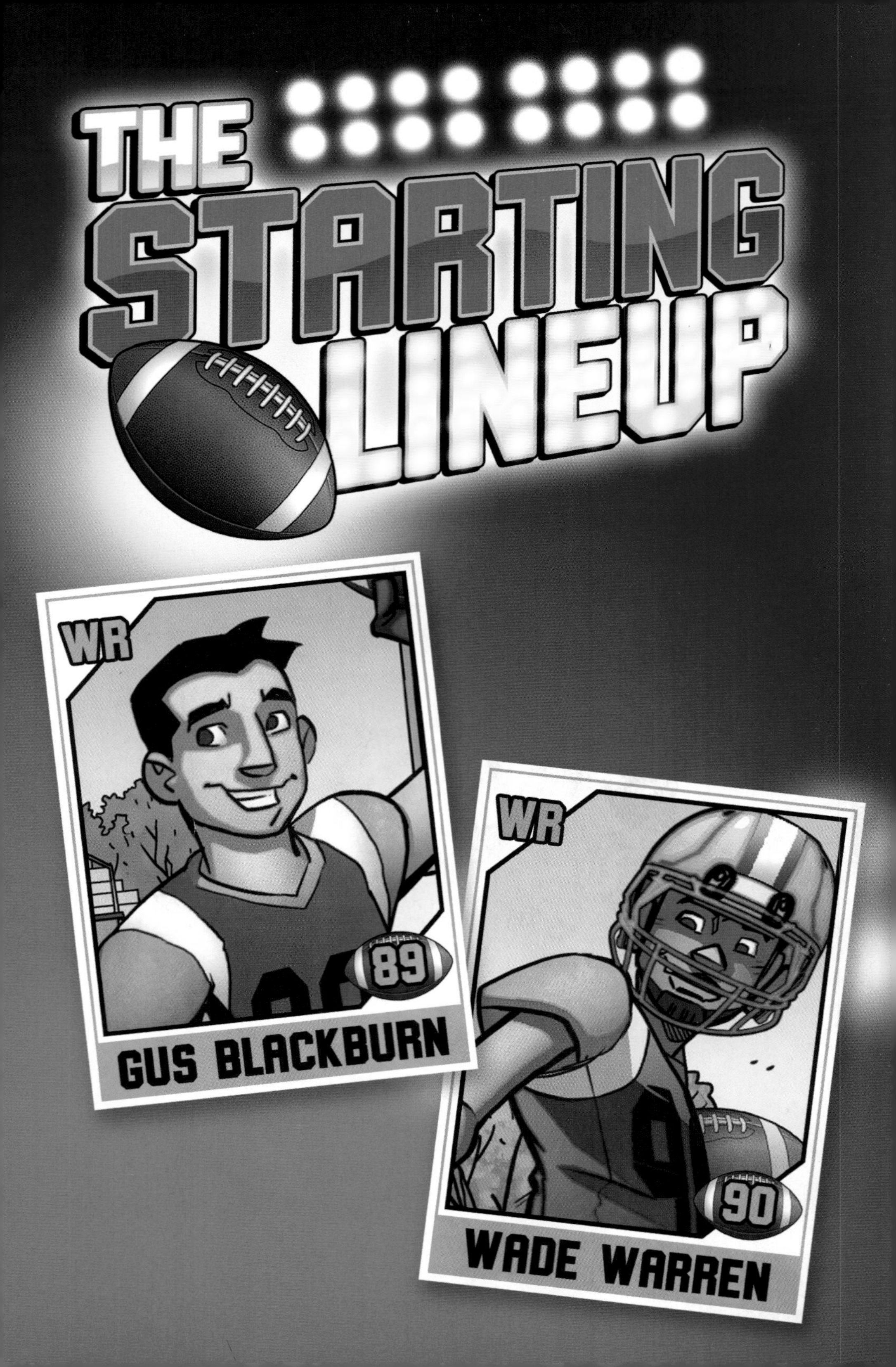
THE STARTING LINEUP
WR
89
GUS BLACKBURN
WR
90
WADE WARREN

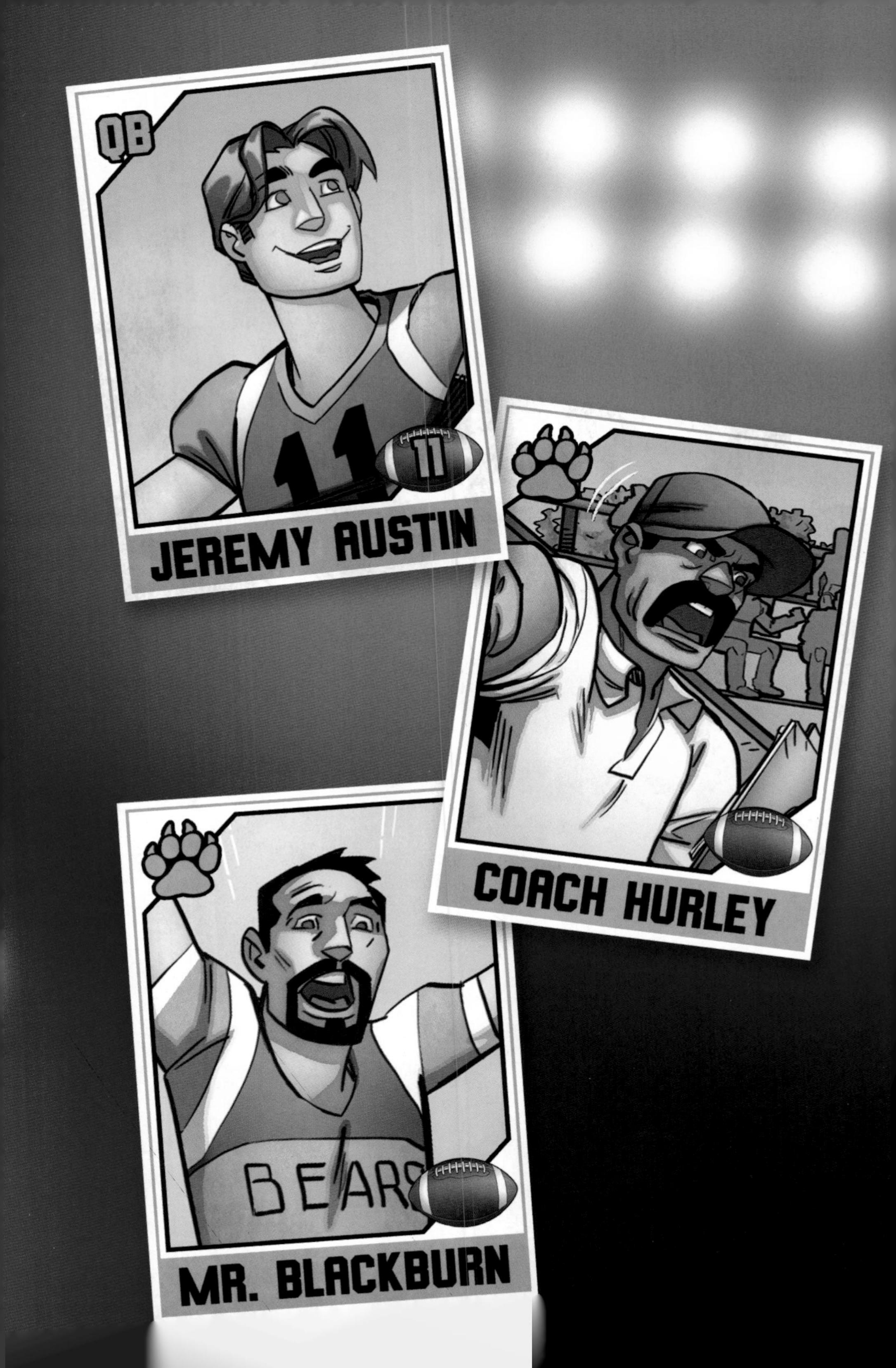
QB
11
11
JEREMY AUSTIN
COACH HURLEY
BEARS
MR. BLACKBURN

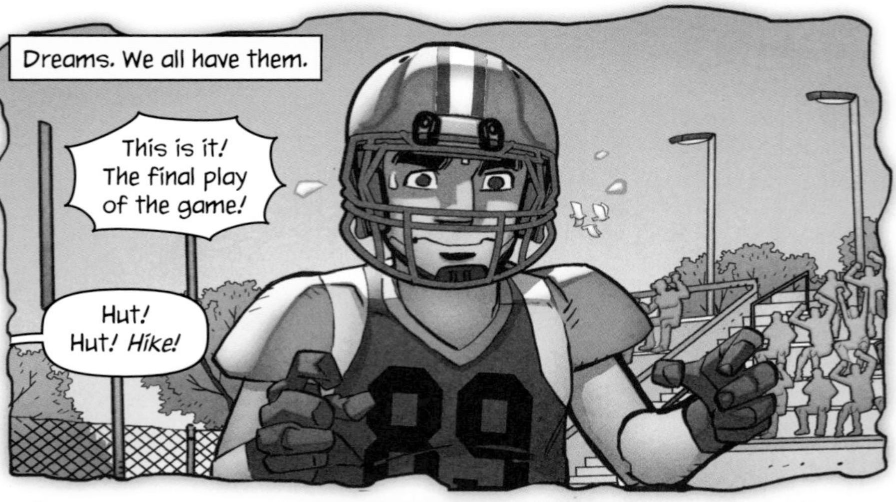
Dreams. We all have them.
This is it! The final play of the game!
Hut! Hut! *Hike!*

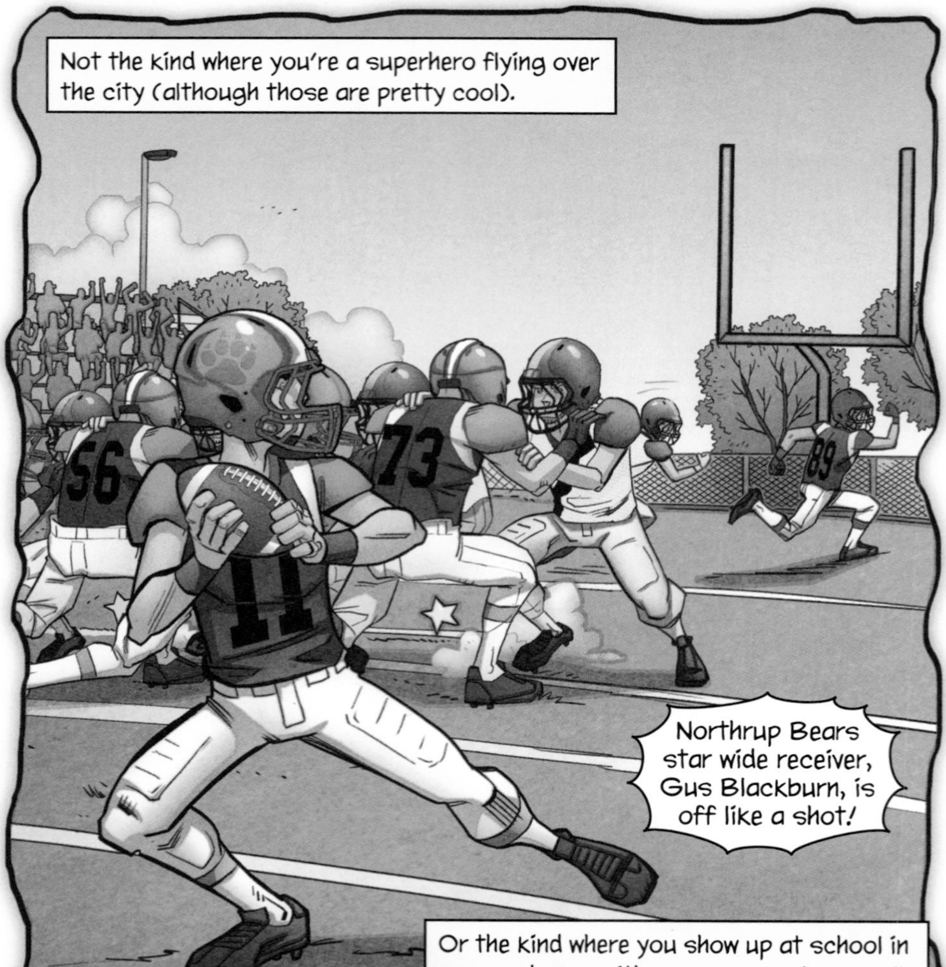
Not the kind where you're a superhero flying over the city (although those are pretty cool).
Northrup Bears star wide receiver, Gus Blackburn, is off like a shot!
Or the kind where you show up at school in your underwear (those are . . . not so cool).

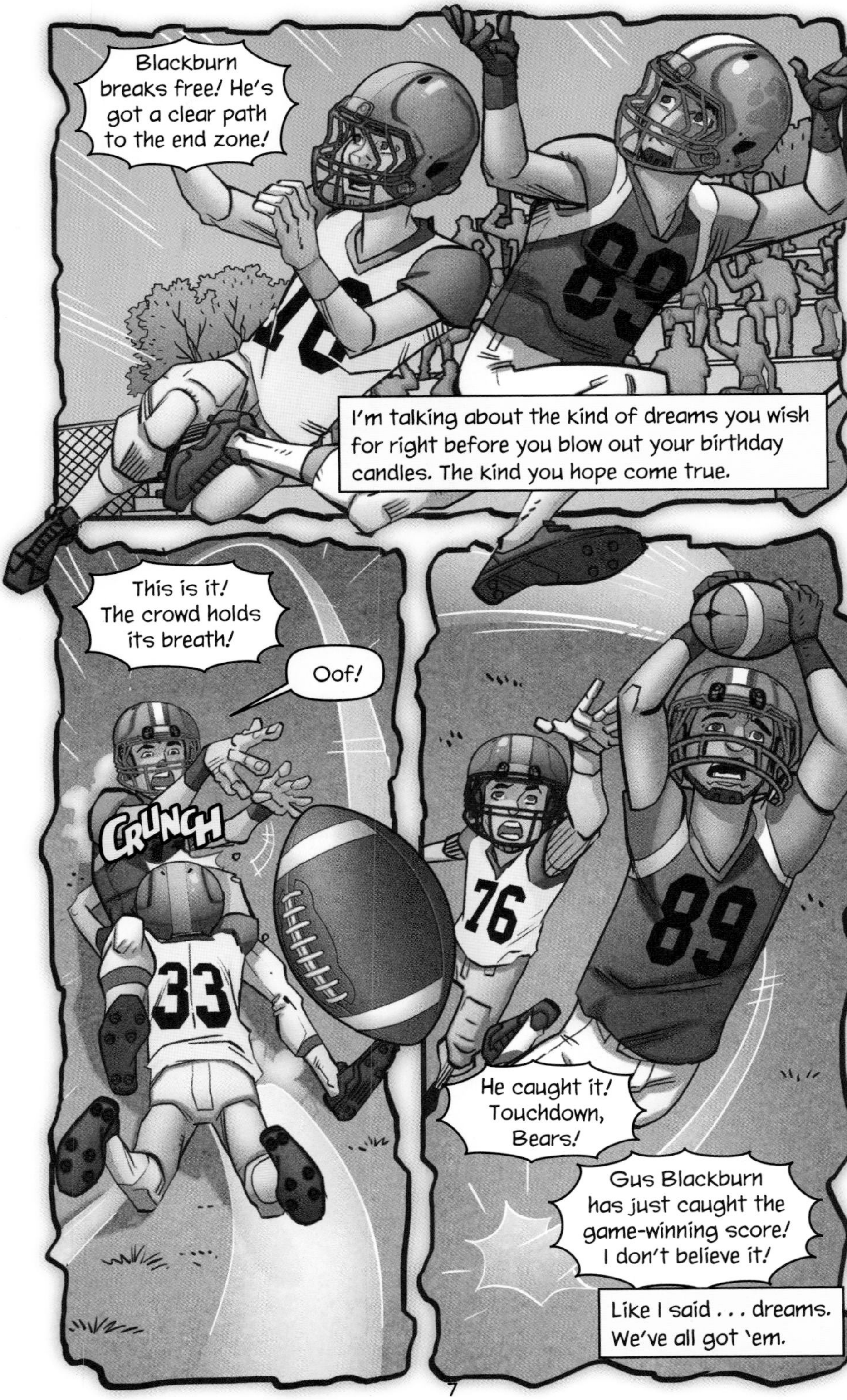
Blackburn breaks free! He's got a clear path to the end zone!
I'm talking about the kind of dreams you wish for right before you blow out your birthday candles. The kind you hope come true.
This is it! The crowd holds its breath!
Oof!
CRUNCH
He caught it! Touchdown, Bears!
Gus Blackburn has just caught the game-winning score! I don't believe it!
Like I said . . . dreams. We've all got 'em.

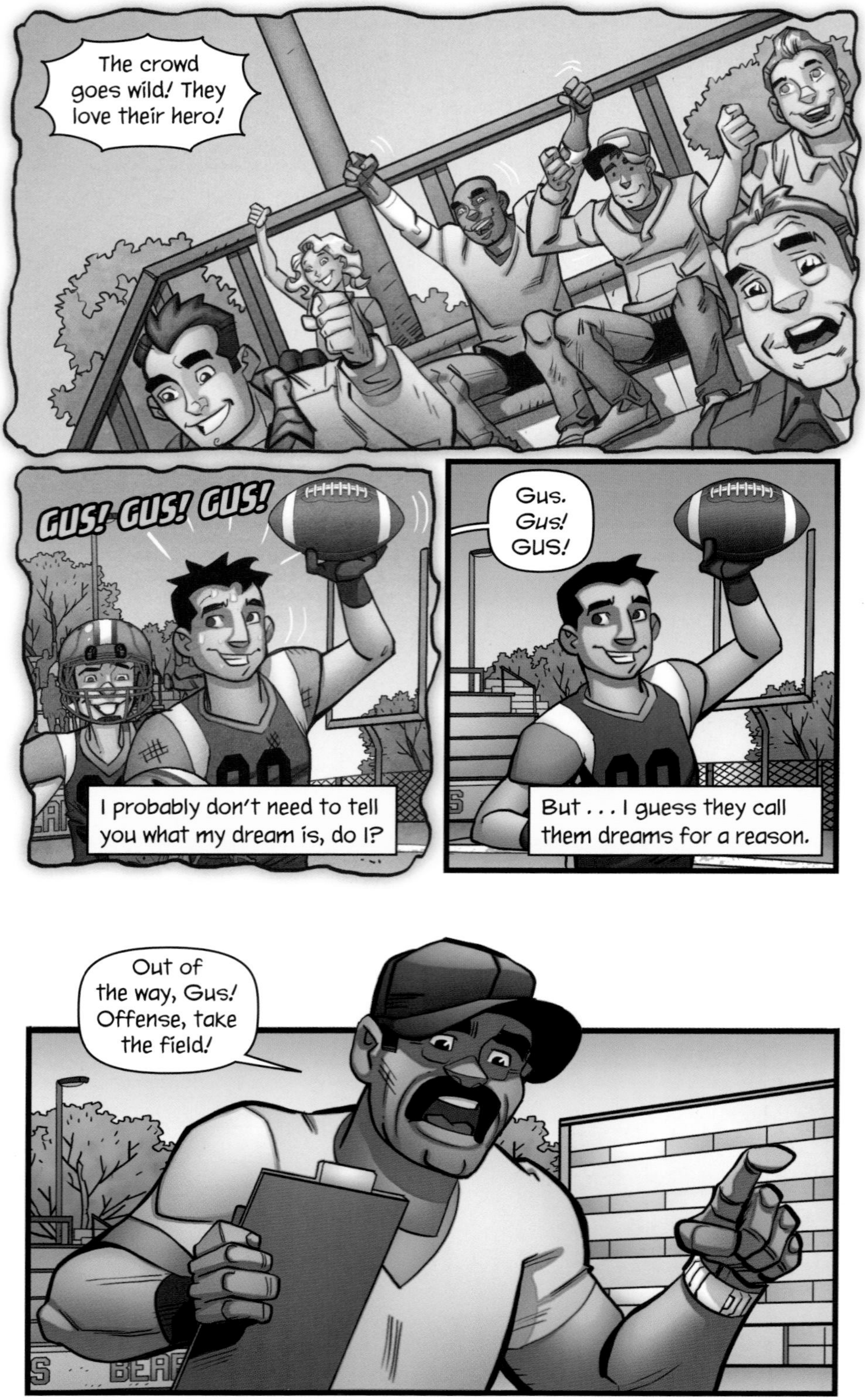
The crowd goes wild! They love their hero!
GUS! GUS! GUS!
I probably don't need to tell you what my dream is, do I?
Gus. Gus! GUS!
But . . . I guess they call them dreams for a reason.
Out of the way, Gus! Offense, take the field!

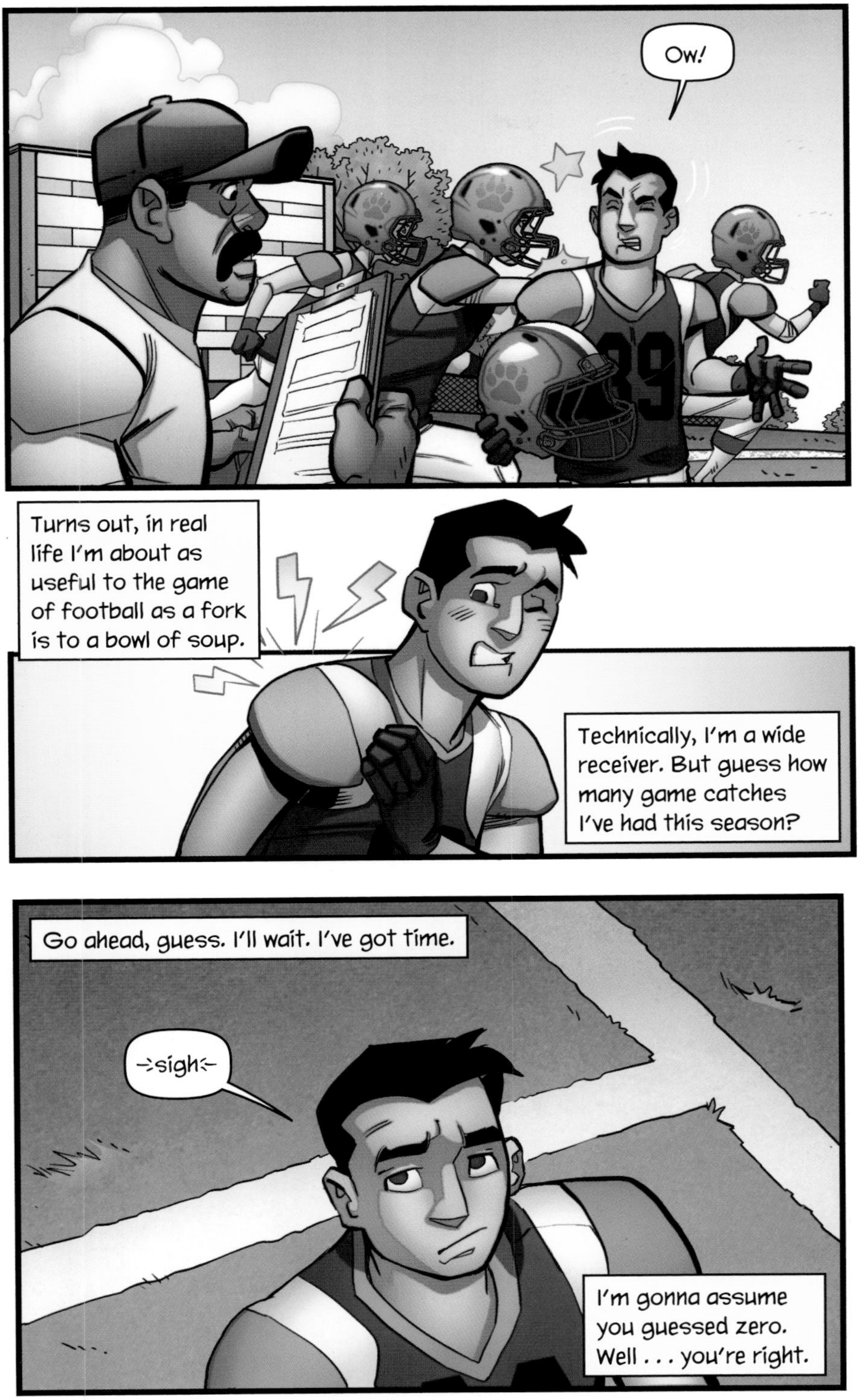
Ow!
Turns out, in real life I'm about as useful to the game of football as a fork is to a bowl of soup.
Technically, I'm a wide receiver. But guess how many game catches I've had this season?
Go ahead, guess. I'll wait. I've got time.
-sigh-
I'm gonna assume you guessed zero. Well . . . you're right.

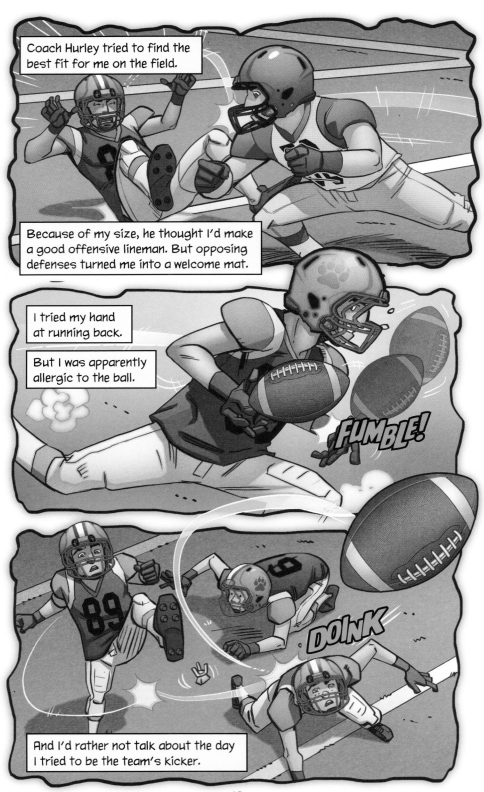

Coach Hurley tried to find the best fit for me on the field.

Because of my size, he thought I'd make a good offensive lineman. But opposing defenses turned me into a welcome mat.

I tried my hand at running back.

But I was apparently allergic to the ball.

FUMBLE!

DOINK

And I'd rather not talk about the day I tried to be the team's kicker.

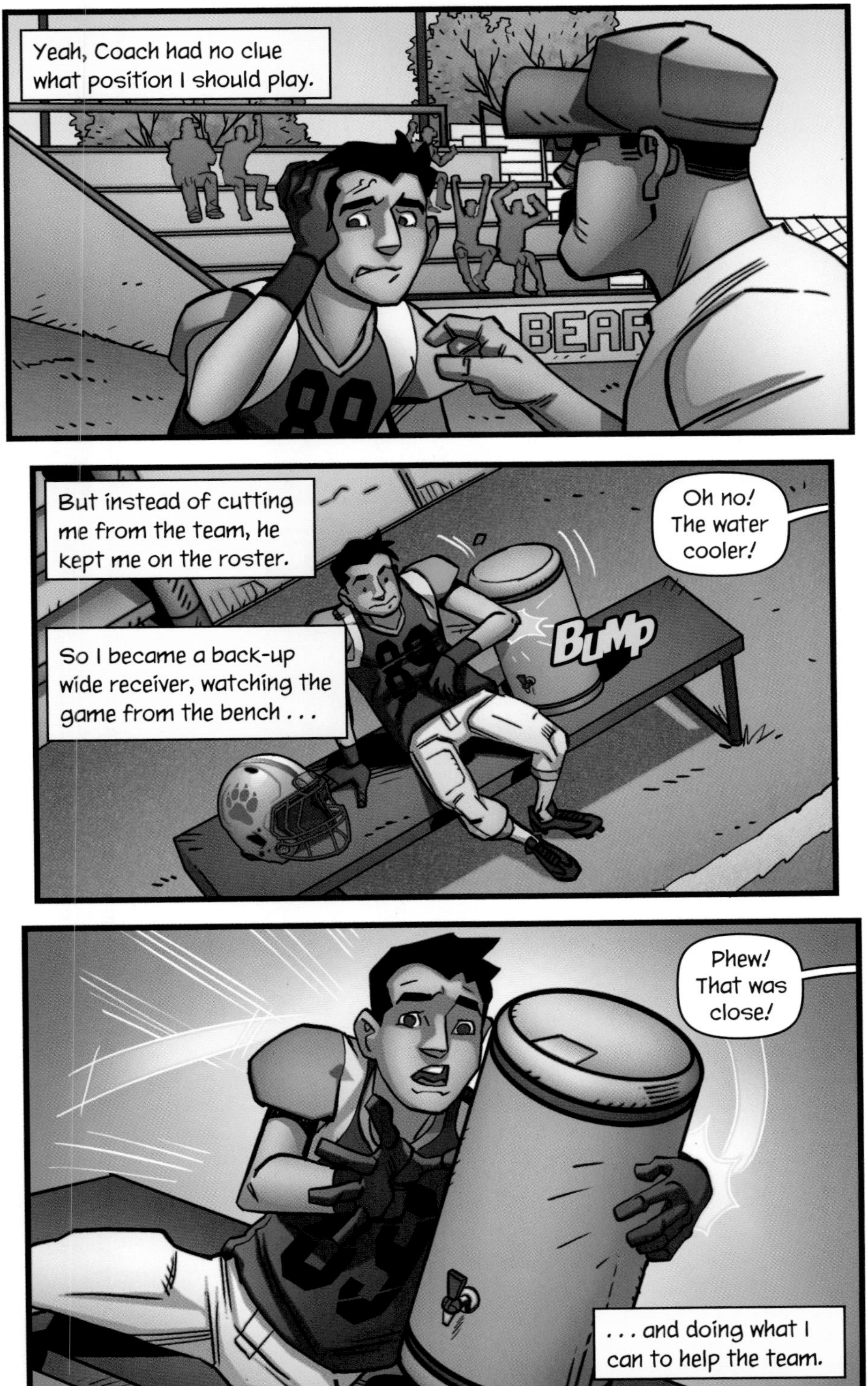
Yeah, Coach had no clue what position I should play.
BEAR
But instead of cutting me from the team, he kept me on the roster.
So I became a back-up wide receiver, watching the game from the bench . . .
Oh no! The water cooler!
BUMP
Phew! That was close!
. . . and doing what I can to help the team.

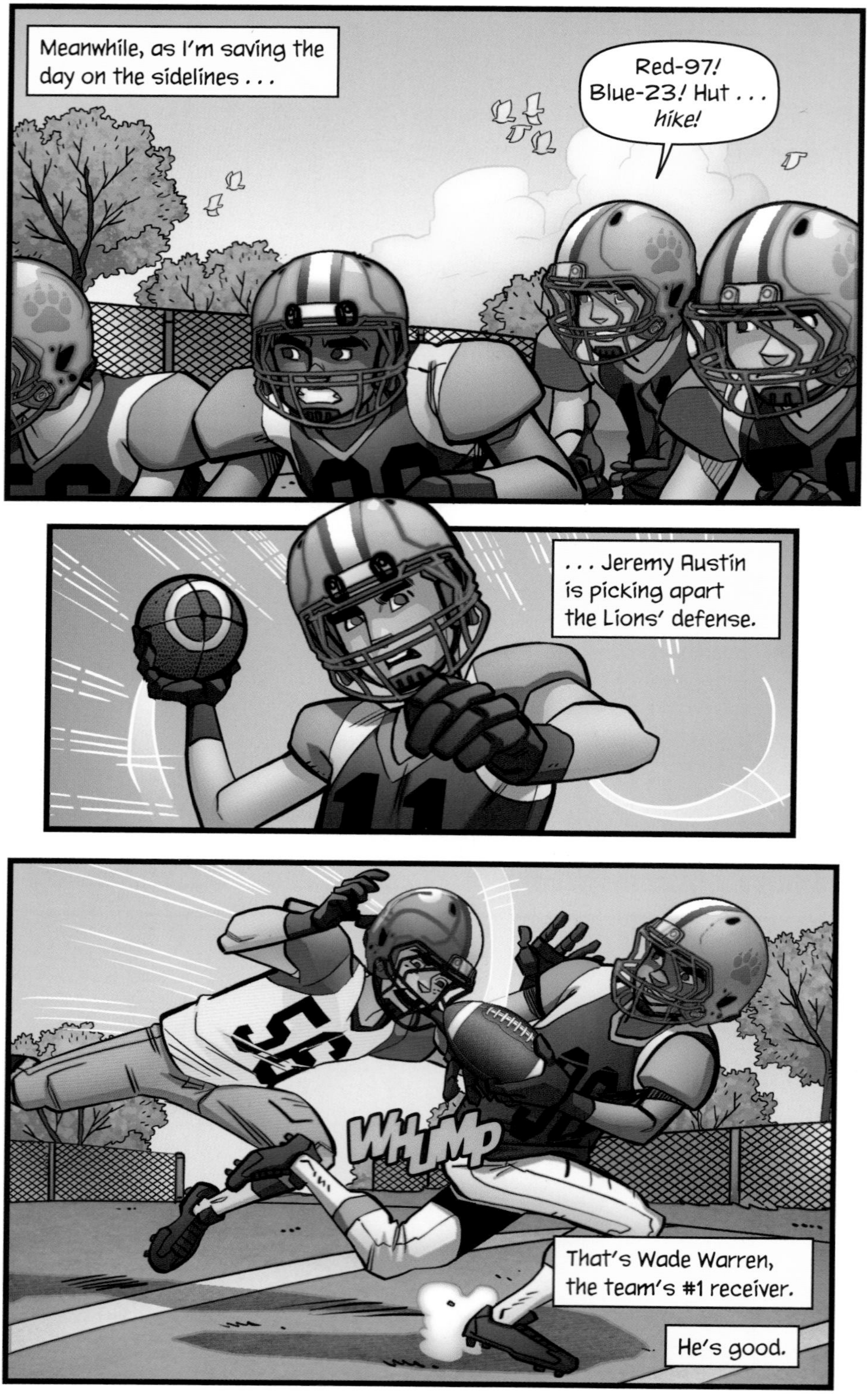
Meanwhile, as I'm saving the day on the sidelines . . .
Red-97! Blue-23! Hut . . . hike!
. . . Jeremy Austin is picking apart the Lions' defense.
WHUMP
That's Wade Warren, the team's #1 receiver.
He's good.

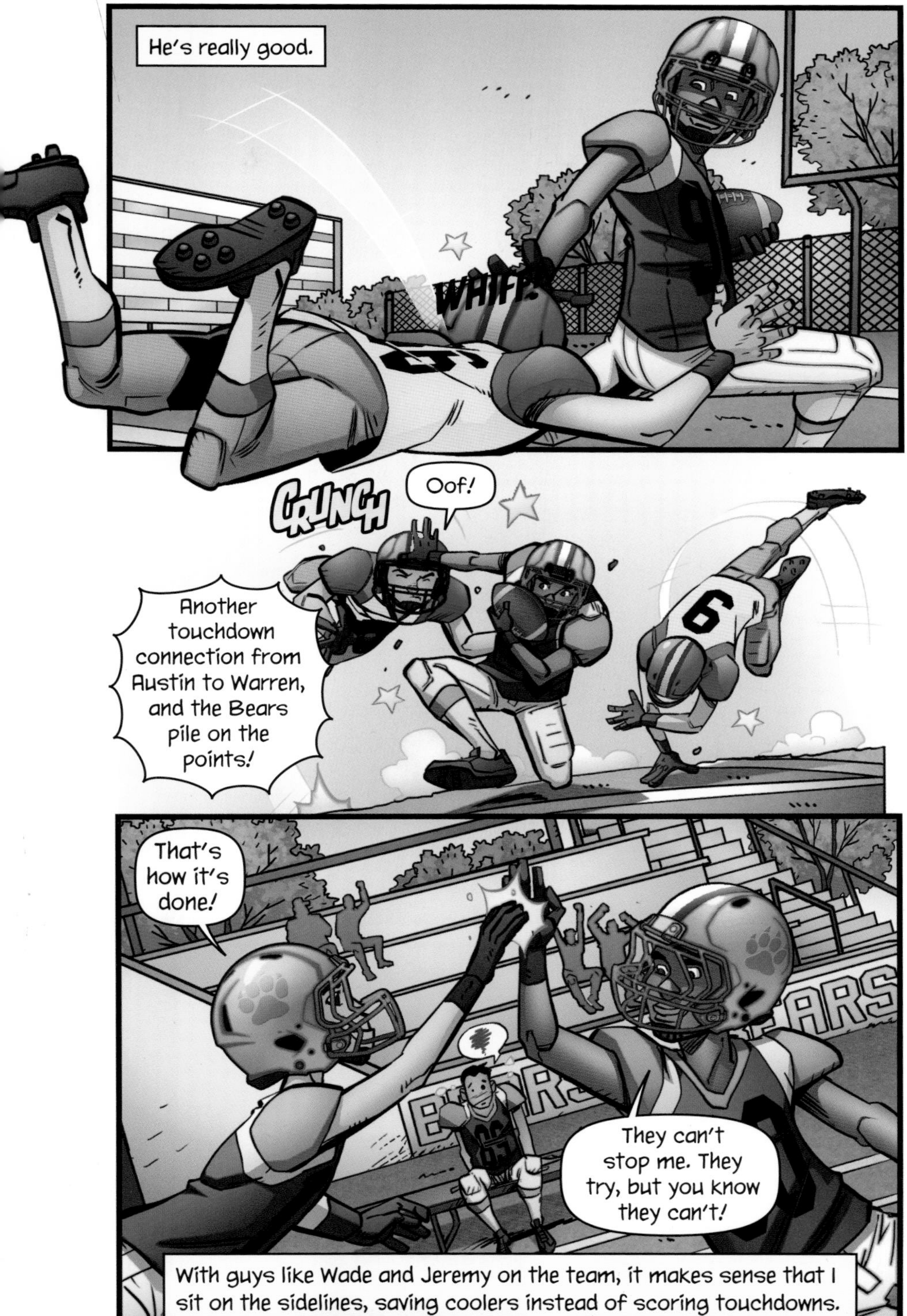
He's really good.
WHIFF!
CRUNCH
Oof!
Another touchdown connection from Austin to Warren, and the Bears pile on the points!
That's how it's done!
They can't stop me. They try, but you know they can't!
With guys like Wade and Jeremy on the team, it makes sense that I sit on the sidelines, saving coolers instead of scoring touchdowns.

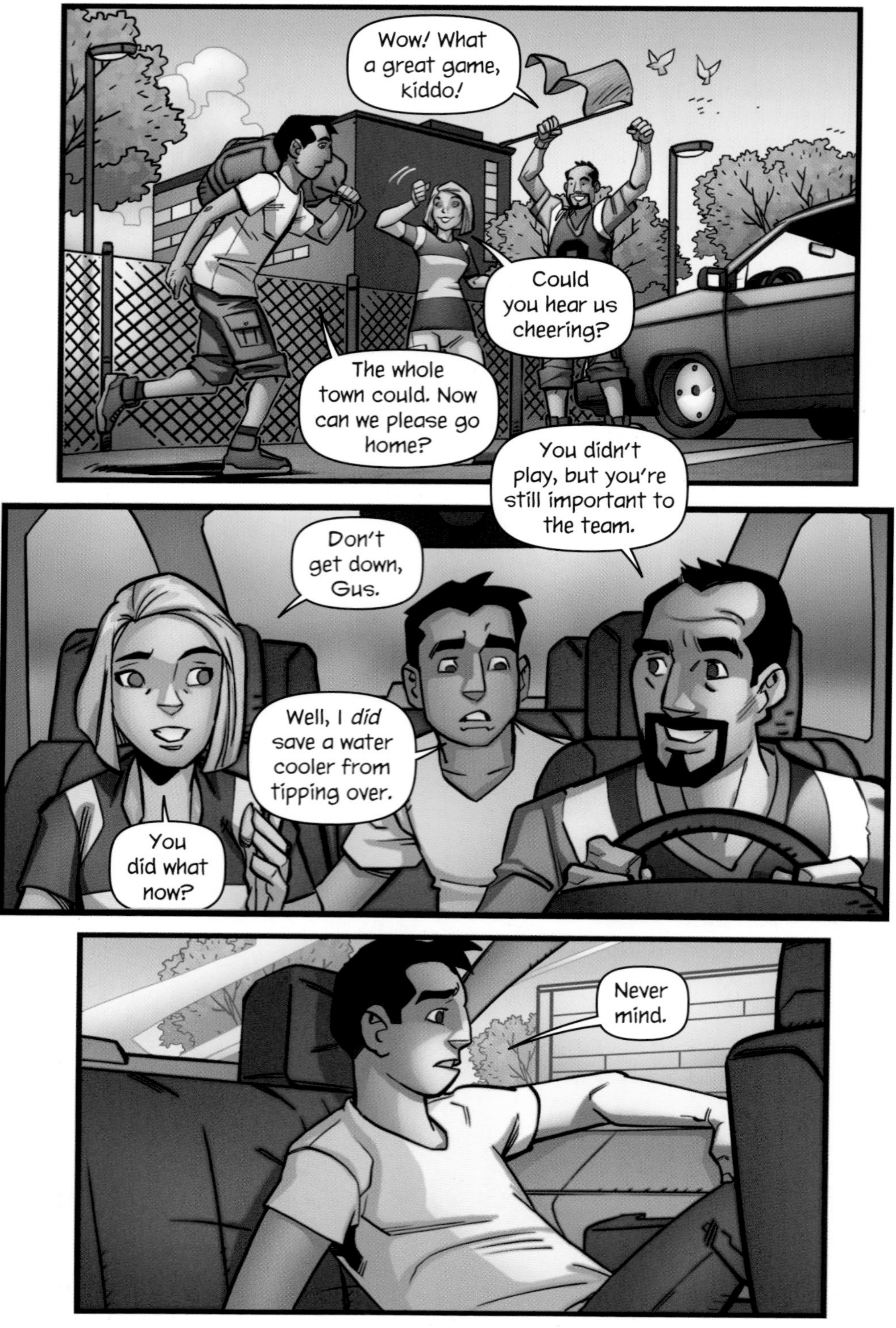
Wow! What a great game, kiddo!
Could you hear us cheering?
The whole town could. Now can we please go home?
You didn't play, but you're still important to the team.
Don't get down, Gus.
Well, I *did* save a water cooler from tipping over.
You did what now?
Never mind.

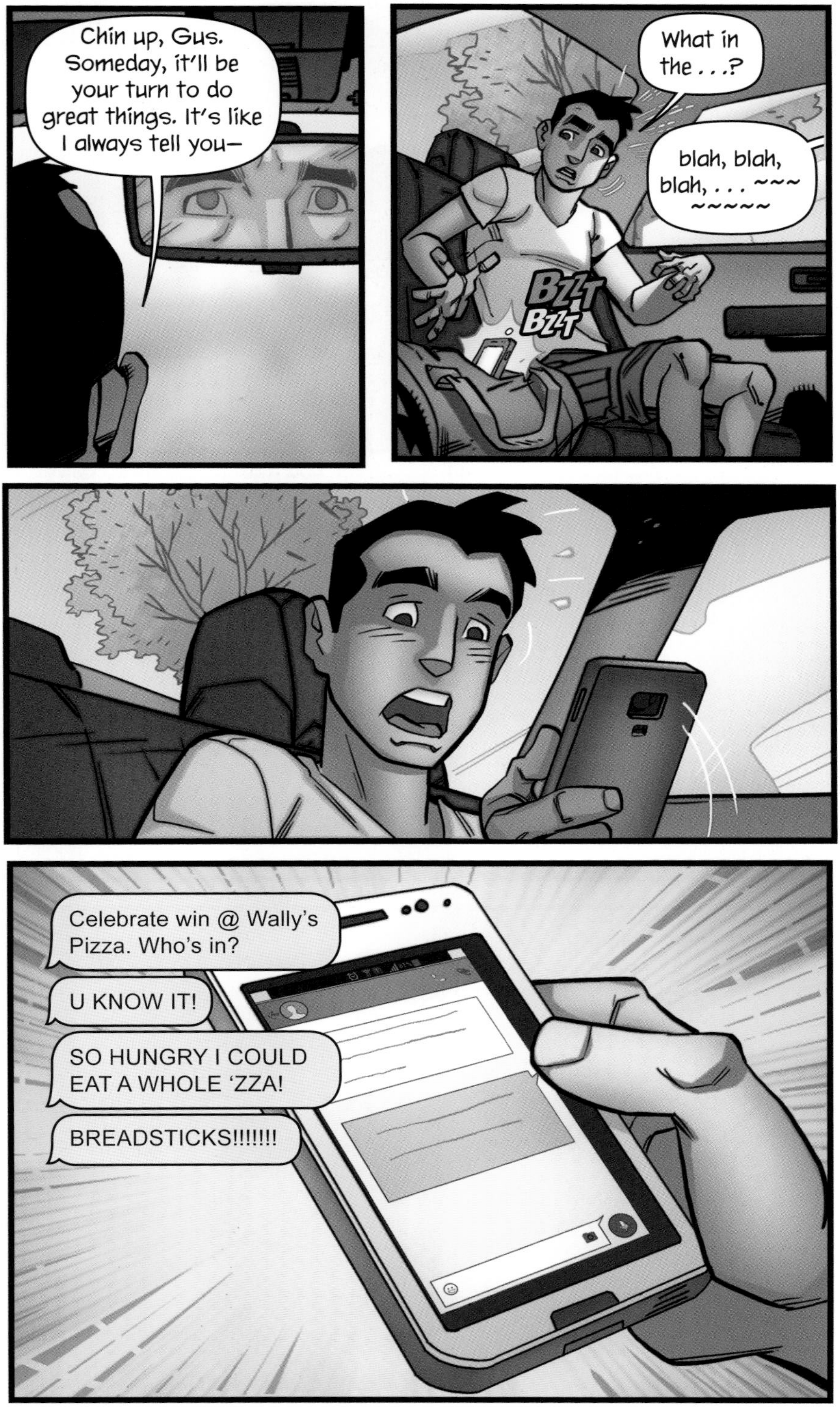
Chin up, Gus. Someday, it'll be your turn to do great things. It's like I always tell you—
What in the . . .?
blah, blah, blah, . . . ~~~ ~~~~~
BZZT BZZT
Celebrate win @ Wally's Pizza. Who's in?
U KNOW IT!
SO HUNGRY I COULD EAT A WHOLE 'ZZA!
BREADSTICKS!!!!!!!

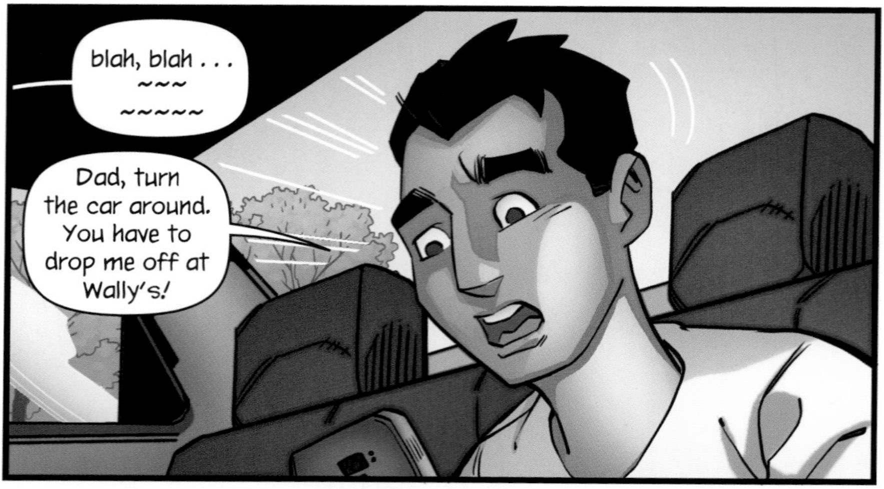
blah, blah . . .
~~~
~~~~~
Dad, turn the car around. You have to drop me off at Wally's!

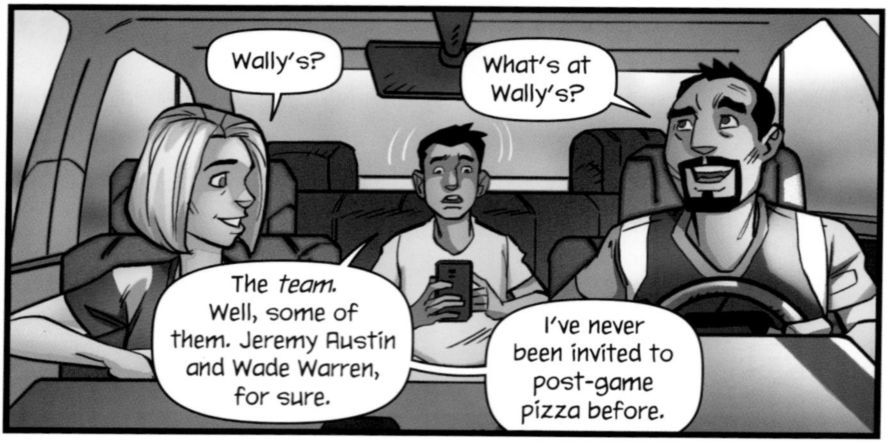
Wally's?
What's at Wally's?
The *team.* Well, some of them. Jeremy Austin and Wade Warren, for sure.
I've never been invited to post-game pizza before.

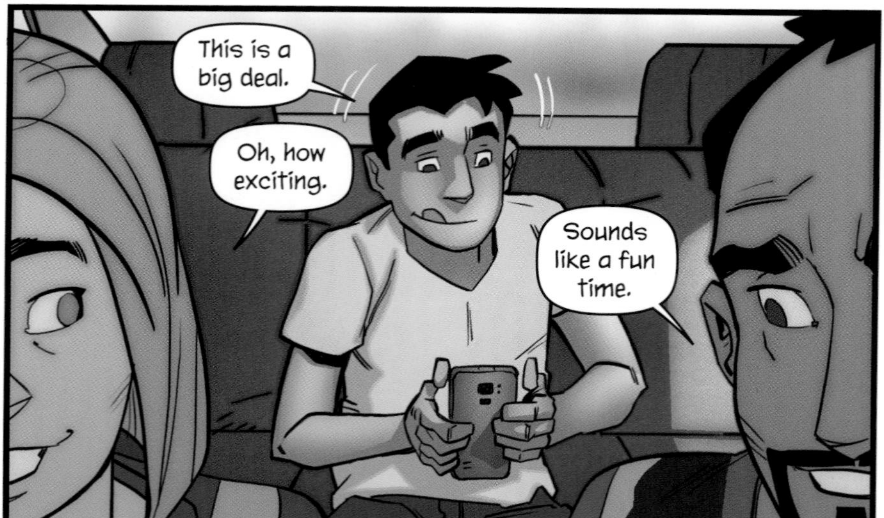
This is a big deal.
Oh, how exciting.
Sounds like a fun time.

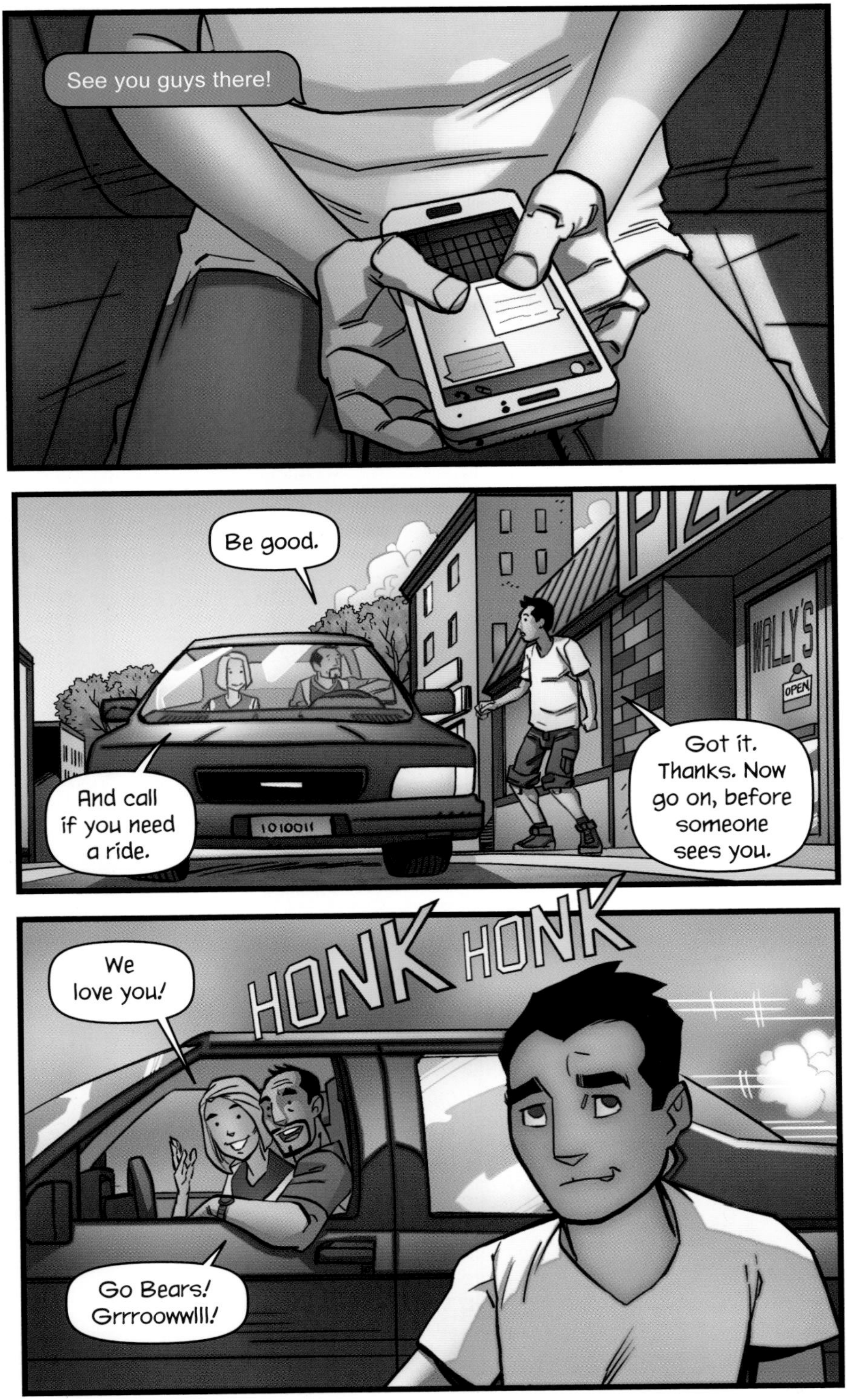
See you guys there!
Be good.
PIZ
WALLY'S
OPEN
1010011
And call if you need a ride.
Got it. Thanks. Now go on, before someone sees you.
HONK HONK
We love you!
Go Bears! Grrroowwlll!

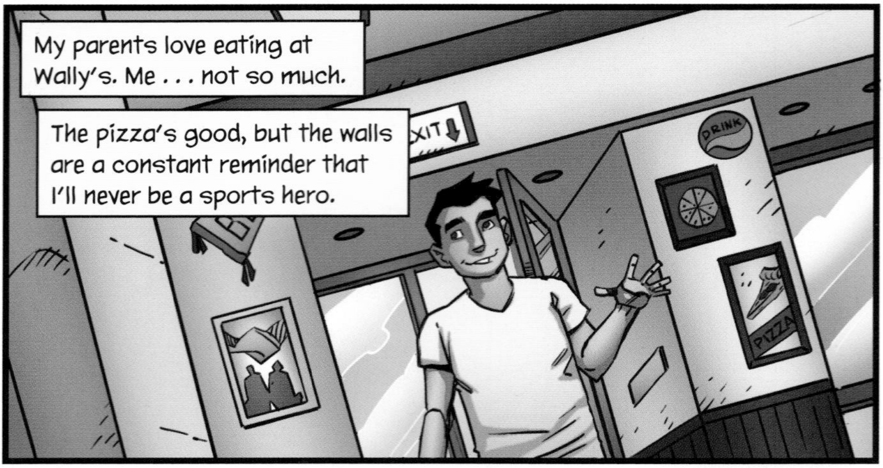
My parents love eating at Wally's. Me . . . not so much.
The pizza's good, but the walls are a constant reminder that I'll never be a sports hero.
XIT
DRINK
PIZZA

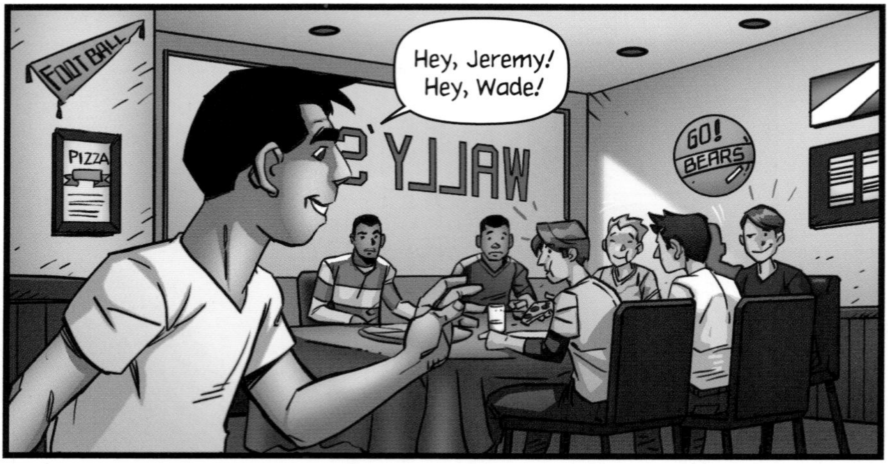
Hey, Jeremy! Hey, Wade!
FOOTBALL
PIZZA
GO! BEARS

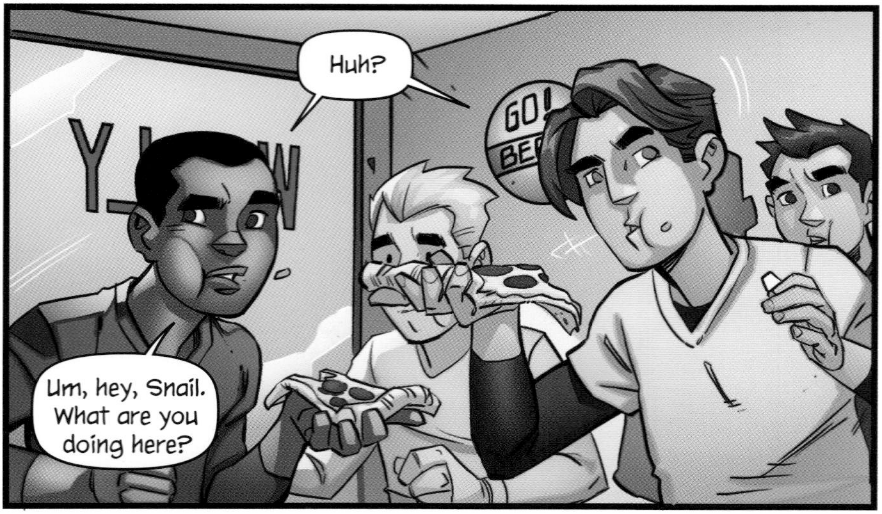
Huh?
Um, hey, Snail. What are you doing here?
GO!

Ugh. Wade calls me Snail all the time, 'cuz I'm not fast. Clever, right?

But I guess it's better than his other nickname for me.

Hey, guys! Did someone invite Humun-*Gus*?

That's the one.

Come on, now. Gus is a part of the team. He's more than welcome.

On the other hand, Jeremy tries to make everyone on the team feel like they're his best friend.

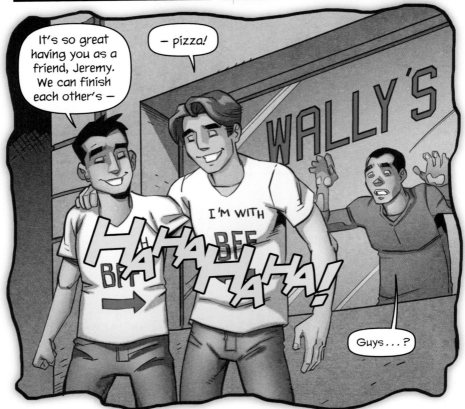

It's so great having you as a friend, Jeremy. We can finish each other's —

— pizza!

WALLY'S

I'M WITH BFF

HAHAHA! HAHA!

Guys . . . ?

Sure, I was more than welcome, but I was hardly a part of the team.

And then — BOOM! — I knocked the running back on his butt!

It was sick!

He's at the ten . . . the five . . . touchdown! The crowd goes wild!

I can't believe I dodged that sack.

I can't believe I caught that pass!

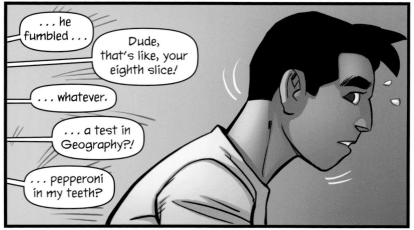

. . . he fumbled . . .

Dude, that's like, your eighth slice!

. . . whatever.

. . . a test in Geography?!

. . . pepperoni in my teeth?

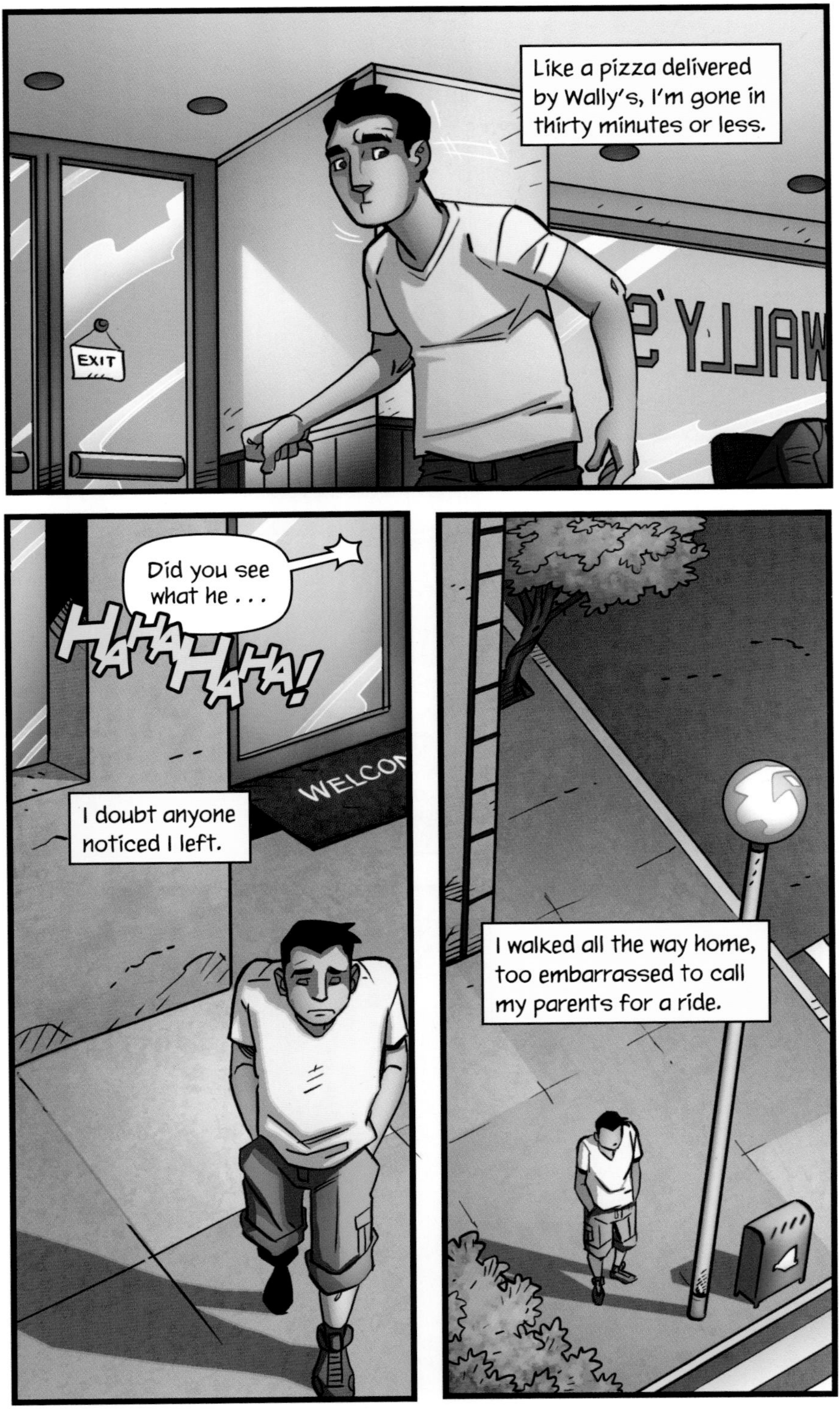
Like a pizza delivered by Wally's, I'm gone in thirty minutes or less.
EXIT
Did you see what he . . .
HAHAHAHAHA!
I doubt anyone noticed I left.
I walked all the way home, too embarrassed to call my parents for a ride.

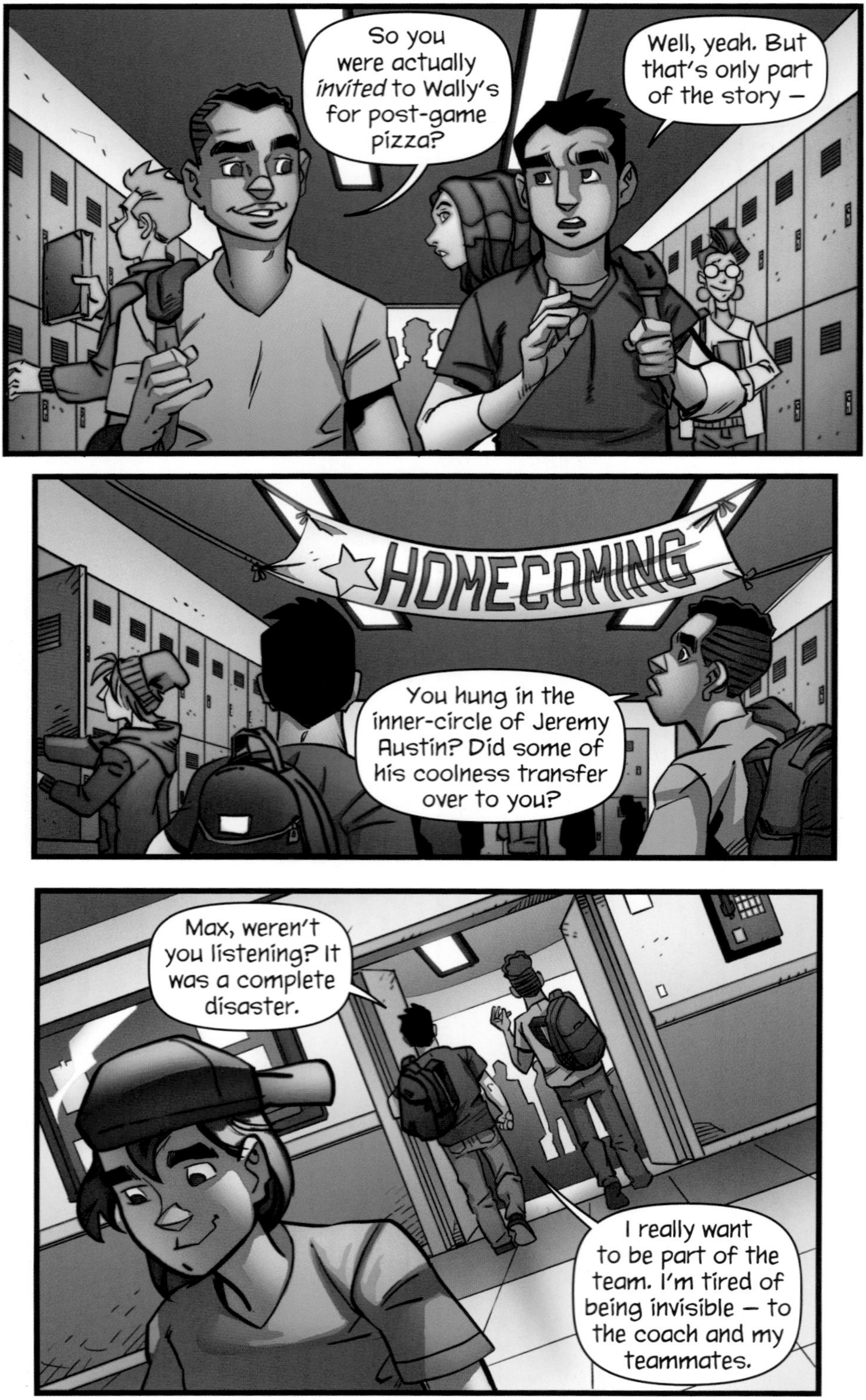
So you were actually *invited* to Wally's for post-game pizza?
Well, yeah. But that's only part of the story —
HOMECOMING
You hung in the inner-circle of Jeremy Austin? Did some of his coolness transfer over to you?
Max, weren't you listening? It was a complete disaster.
I really want to be part of the team. I'm tired of being invisible — to the coach and my teammates.

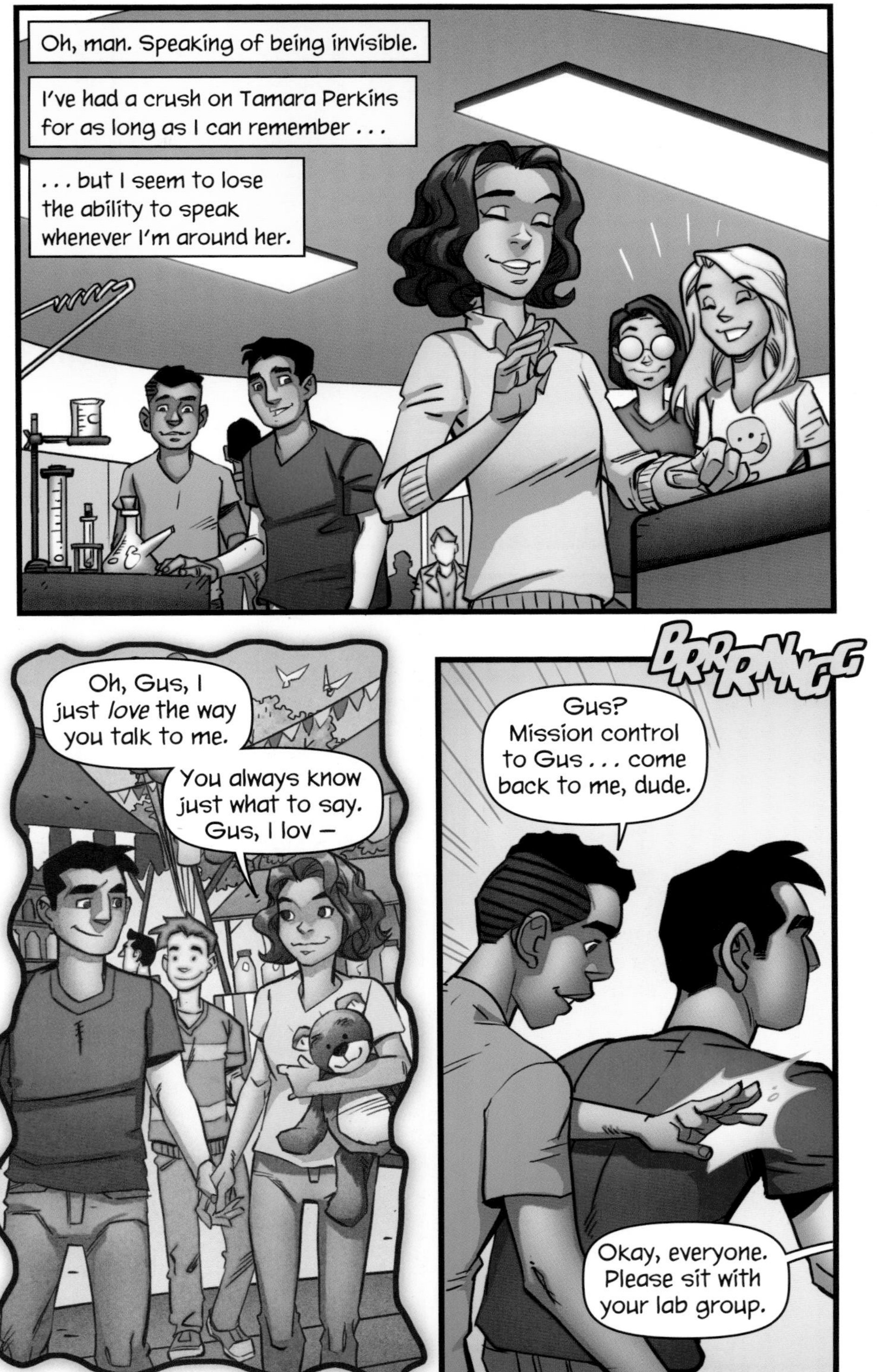

Oh, man. Speaking of being invisible.
I've had a crush on Tamara Perkins for as long as I can remember . . .
. . . but I seem to lose the ability to speak whenever I'm around her.
Oh, Gus, I just *love* the way you talk to me.
You always know just what to say. Gus, I lov –
BRRRRNNGG
Gus? Mission control to Gus . . . come back to me, dude.
Okay, everyone. Please sit with your lab group.

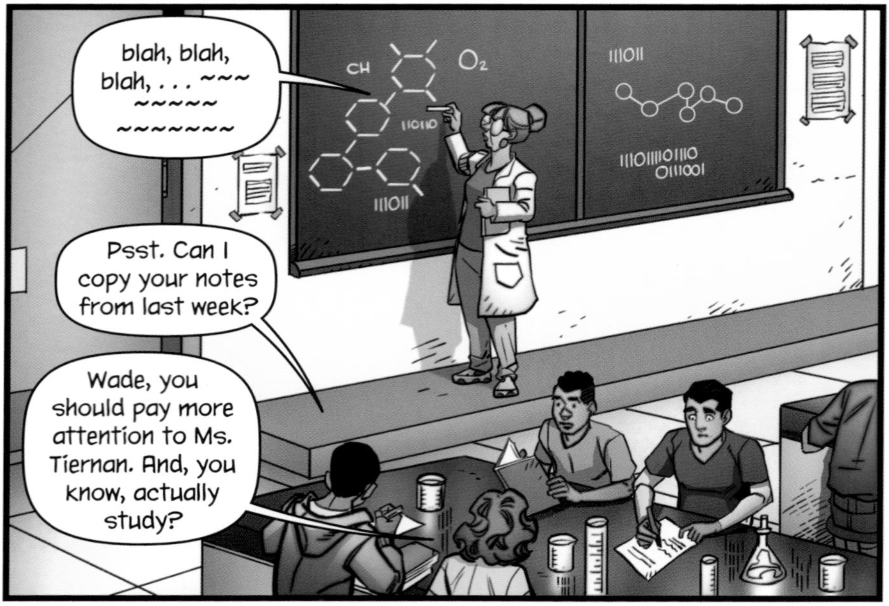
blah, blah, blah, . . . ~~~ ~~~~~ ~~~~~~~
O2
Psst. Can I copy your notes from last week?
Wade, you should pay more attention to Ms. Tiernan. And, you know, actually study?

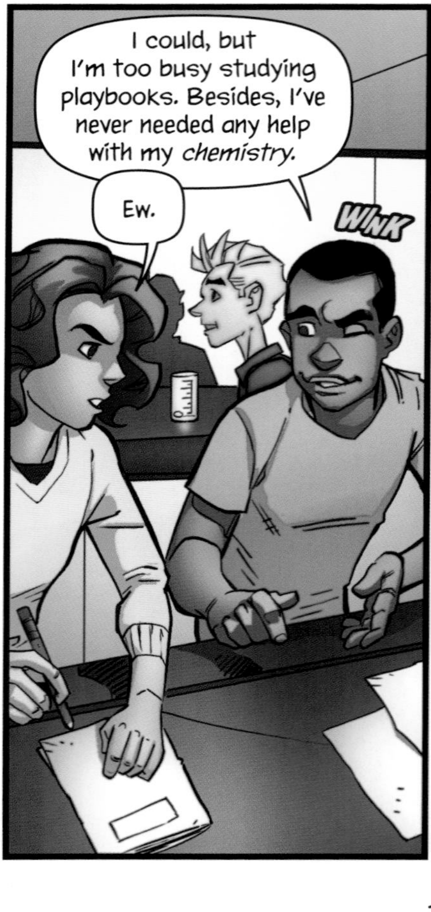
I could, but I'm too busy studying playbooks. Besides, I've never needed any help with my *chemistry.*
Ew.
WINK

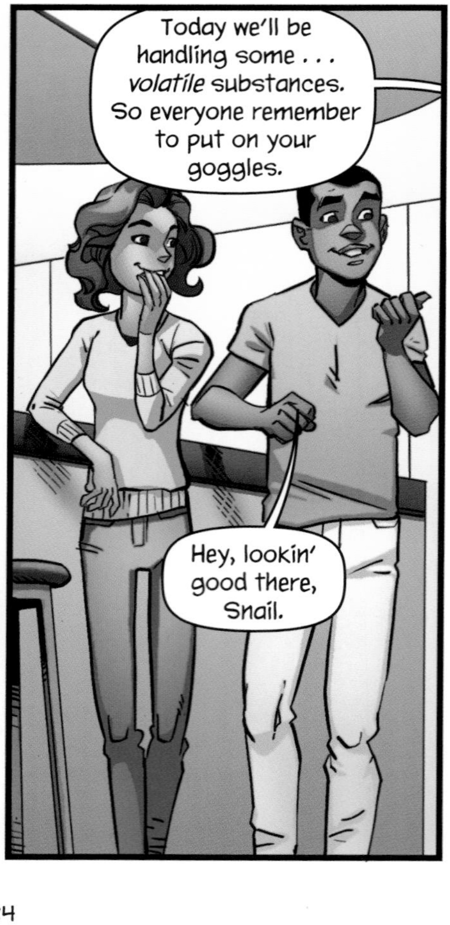
Today we'll be handling some . . . *volatile* substances. So everyone remember to put on your goggles.
Hey, lookin' good there, Snail.

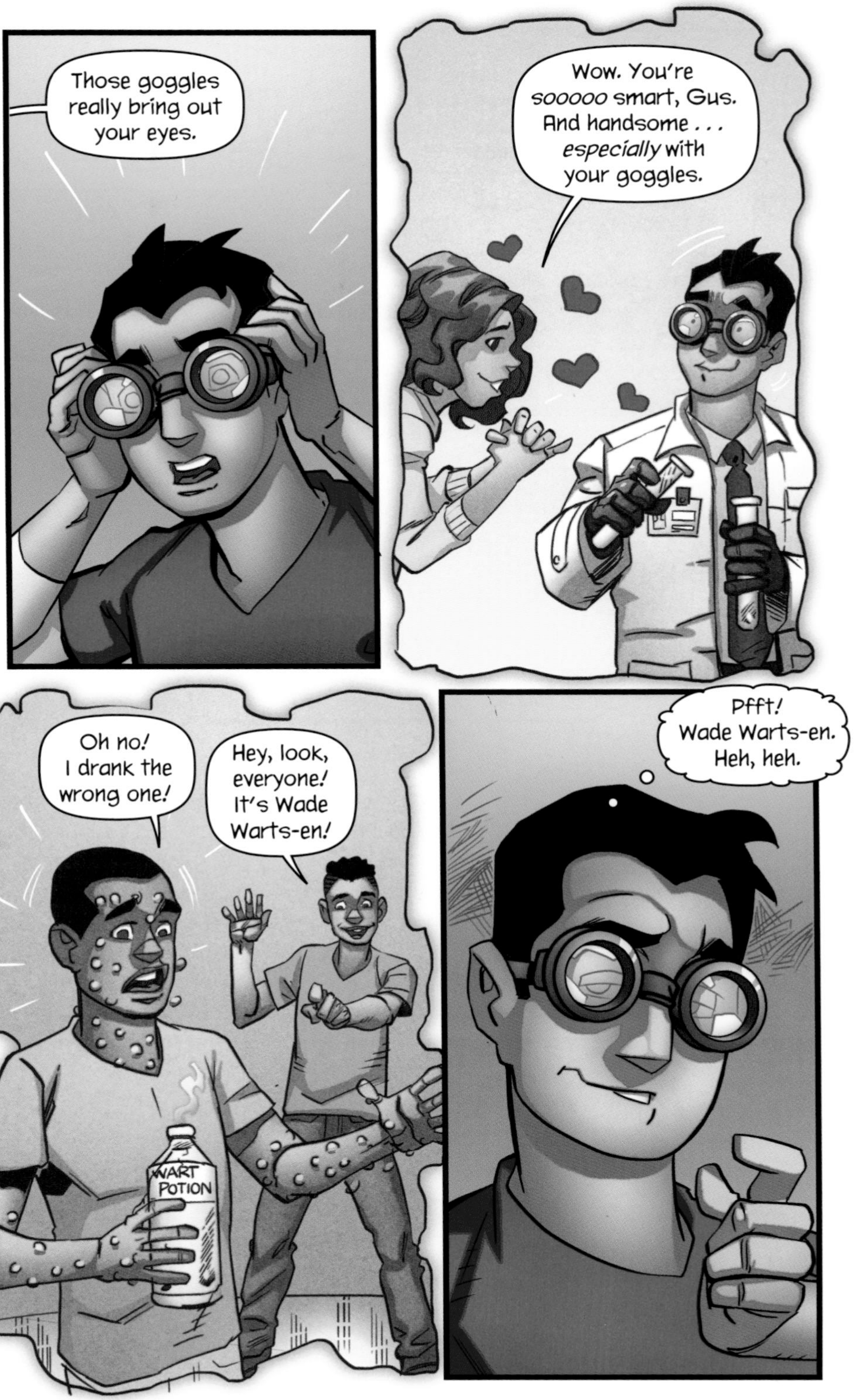
Those goggles really bring out your eyes.
Wow. You're *sooooo* smart, Gus. And handsome . . . *especially* with your goggles.
Oh no! I drank the wrong one!
Hey, look, everyone! It's Wade Warts-en!
WART POTION
Pfft! Wade Warts-en. Heh, heh.

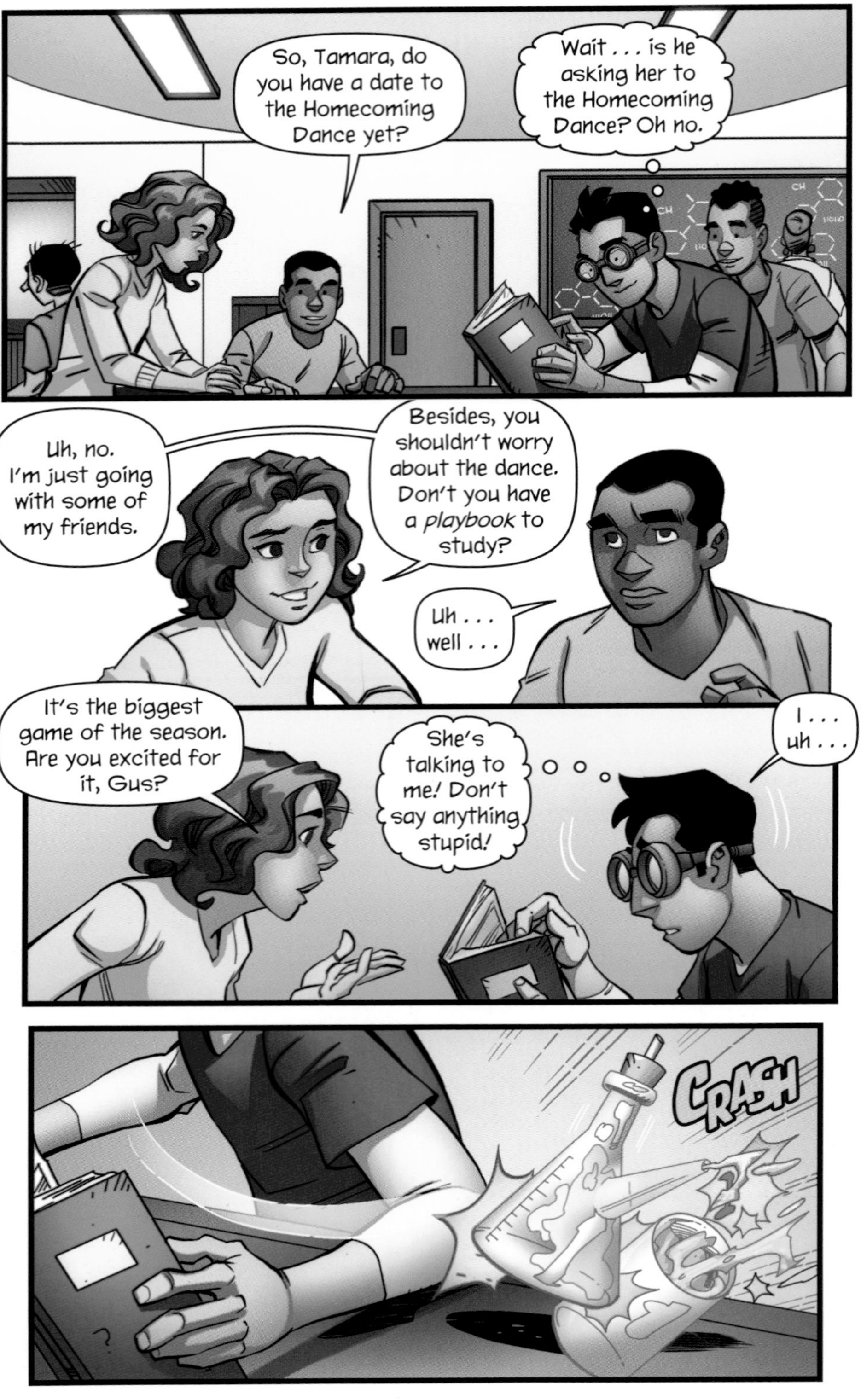
So, Tamara, do you have a date to the Homecoming Dance yet?
Wait . . . is he asking her to the Homecoming Dance? Oh no.
Uh, no. I'm just going with some of my friends.
Besides, you shouldn't worry about the dance. Don't you have a *playbook* to study?
Uh . . . well . . .
It's the biggest game of the season. Are you excited for it, Gus?
She's talking to me! Don't say anything stupid!
I . . . uh . . .
CRASH

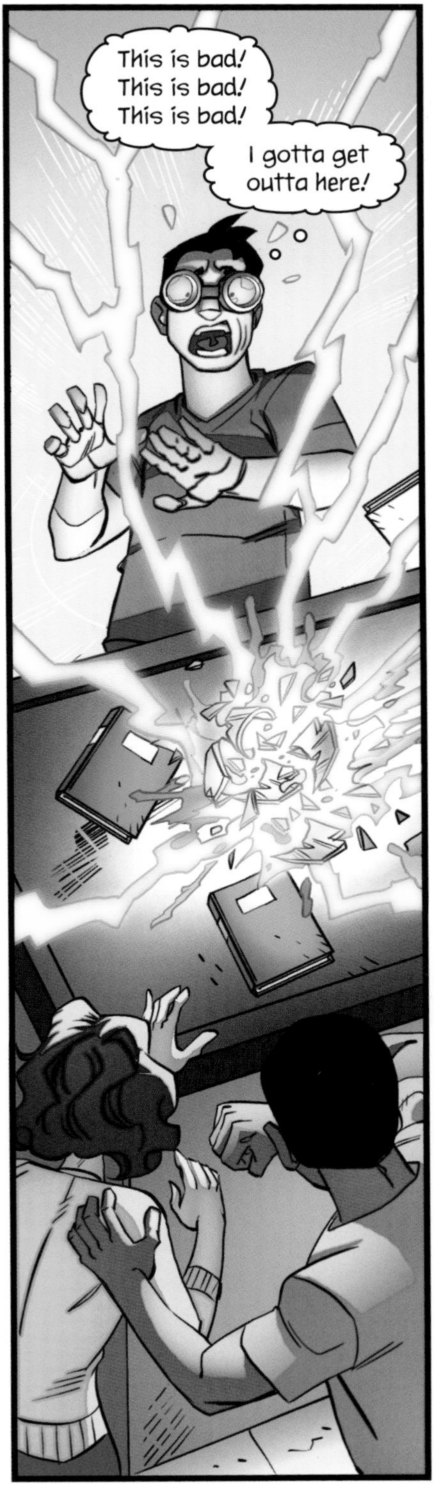
This is bad! This is bad! This is bad!
I gotta get outta here!

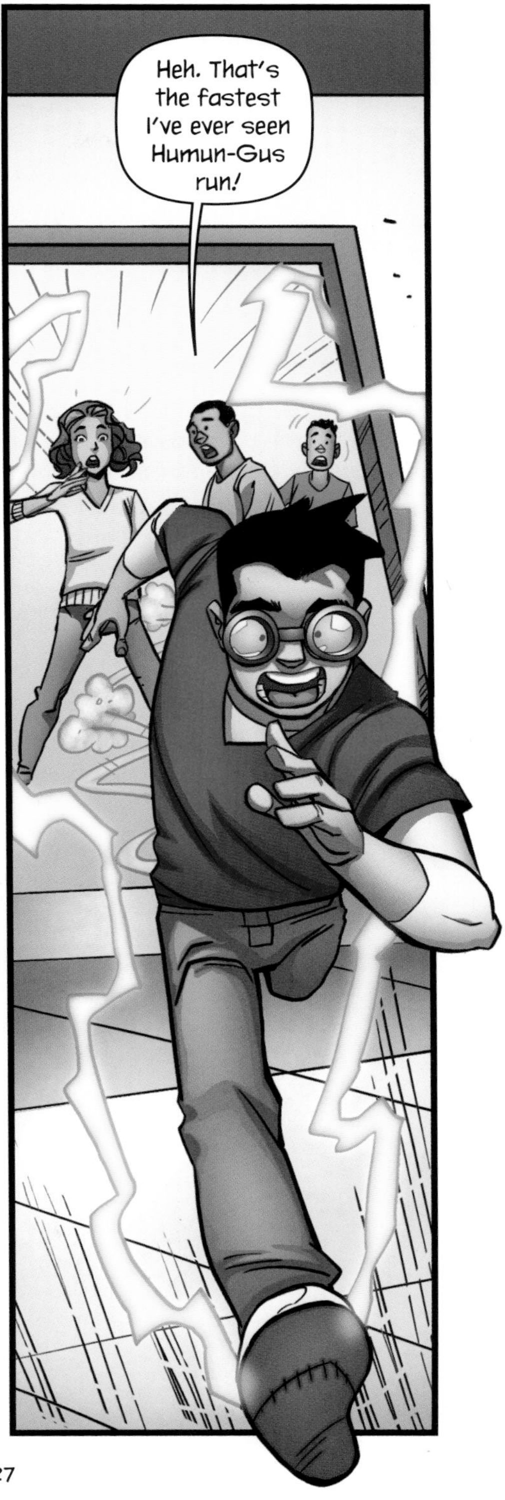
Heh. That's the fastest I've ever seen Humun-Gus run!

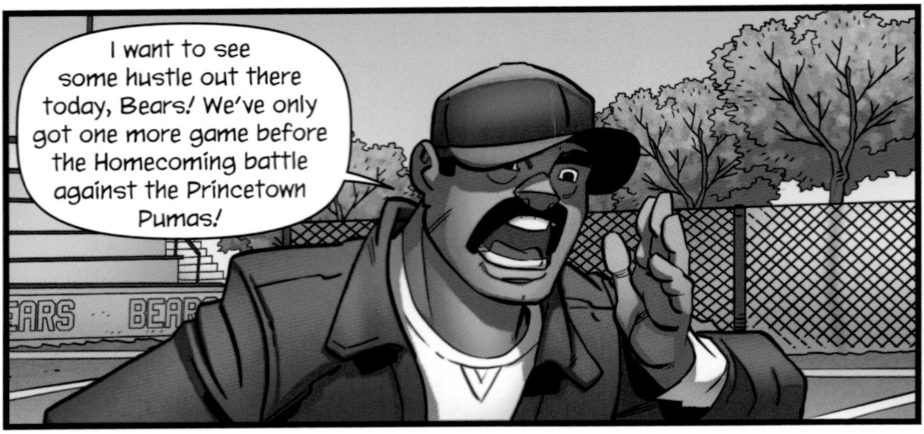
I want to see some hustle out there today, Bears! We've only got one more game before the Homecoming battle against the Princetown Pumas!
BEARS
BEARS

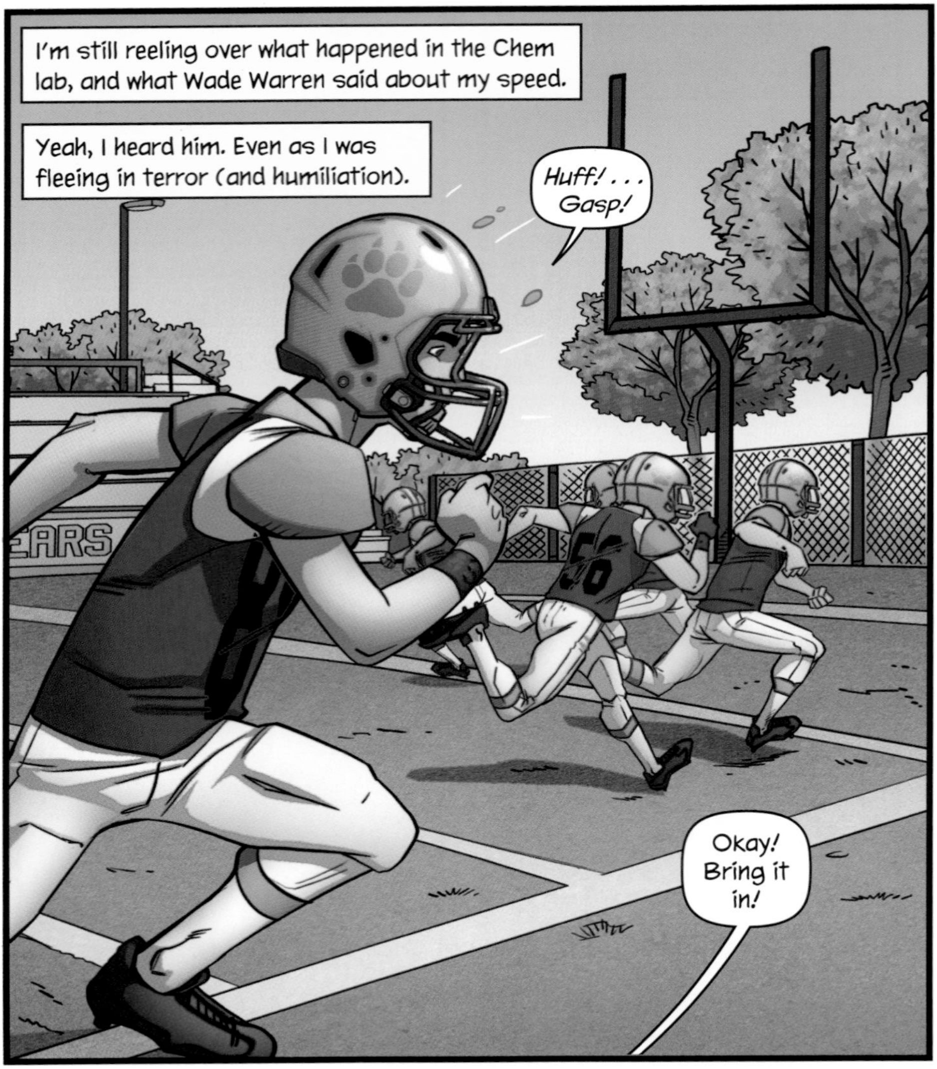
I'm still reeling over what happened in the Chem lab, and what Wade Warren said about my speed.
Yeah, I heard him. Even as I was fleeing in terror (and humiliation).
Huff! . . . Gasp!
EARS
56
Okay! Bring it in!

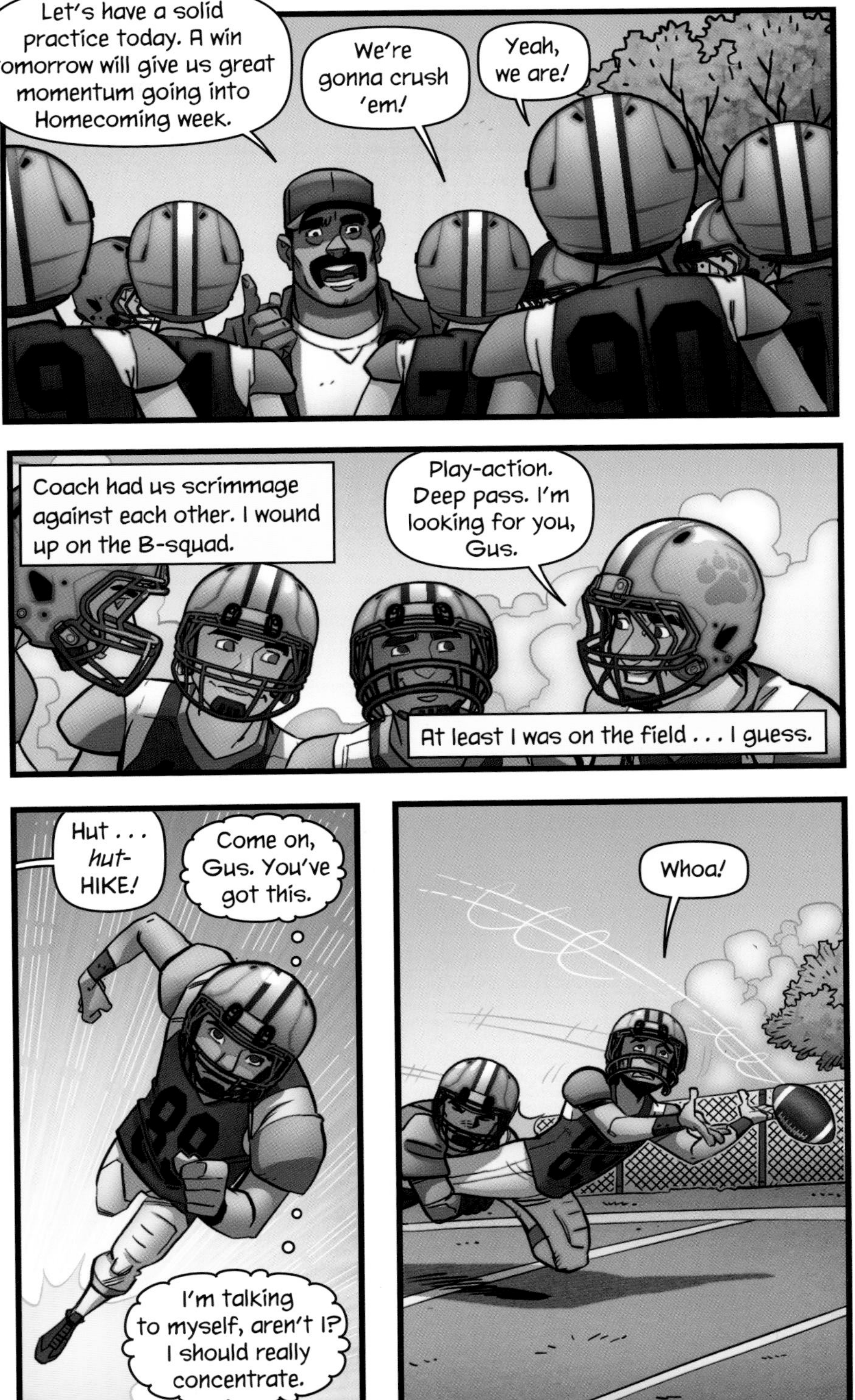
Let's have a solid practice today. A win tomorrow will give us great momentum going into Homecoming week.
We're gonna crush 'em!
Yeah, we are!
Coach had us scrimmage against each other. I wound up on the B-squad.
Play-action. Deep pass. I'm looking for you, Gus.
At least I was on the field . . . I guess.
Hut . . . *hut*-HIKE!
Come on, Gus. You've got this.
I'm talking to myself, aren't I? I should really concentrate.
Whoa!

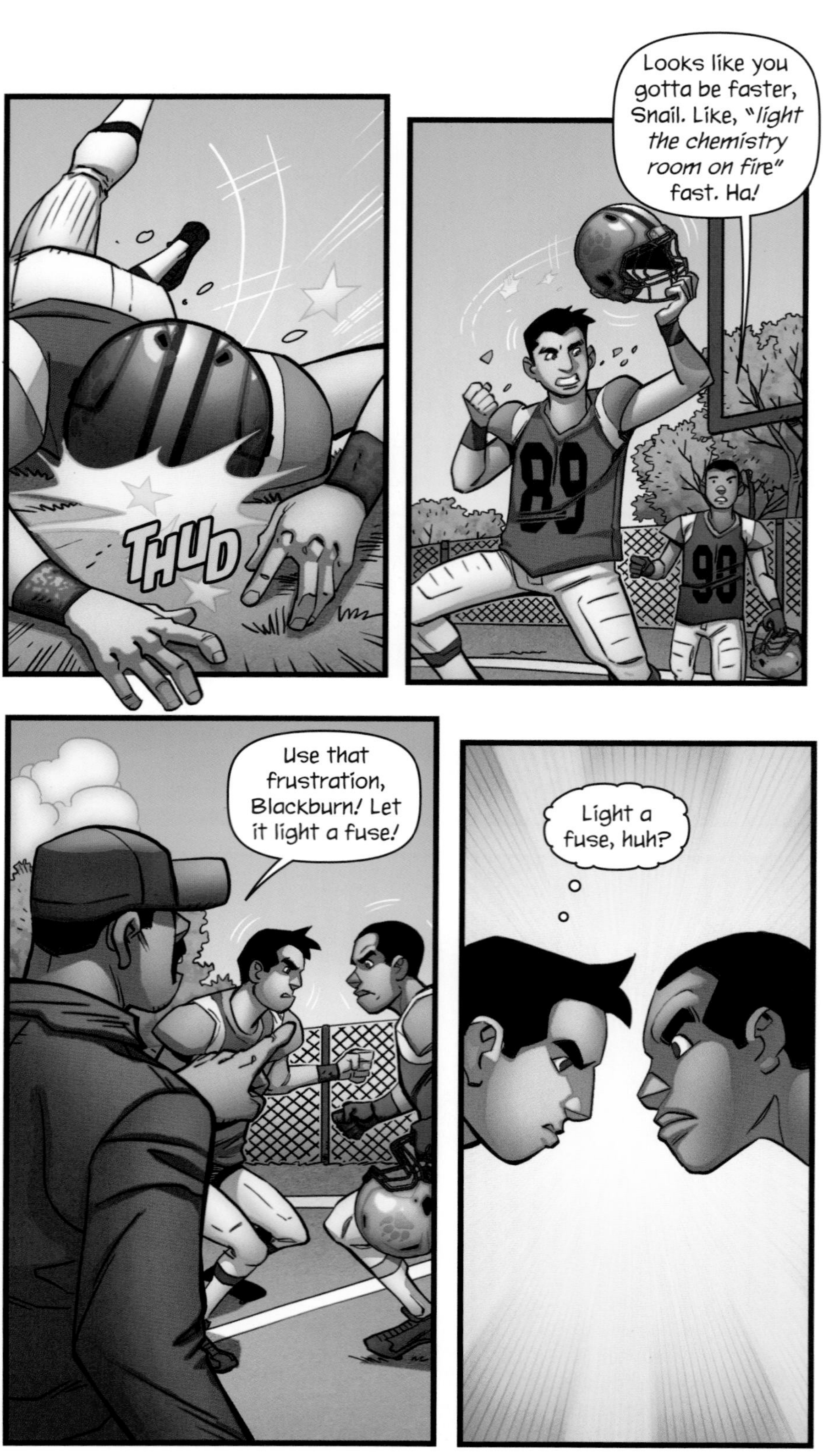
THUD
Looks like you gotta be faster, Snail. Like, "*light the chemistry room on fire*" fast. Ha!
Use that frustration, Blackburn! Let it light a fuse!
Light a fuse, huh?

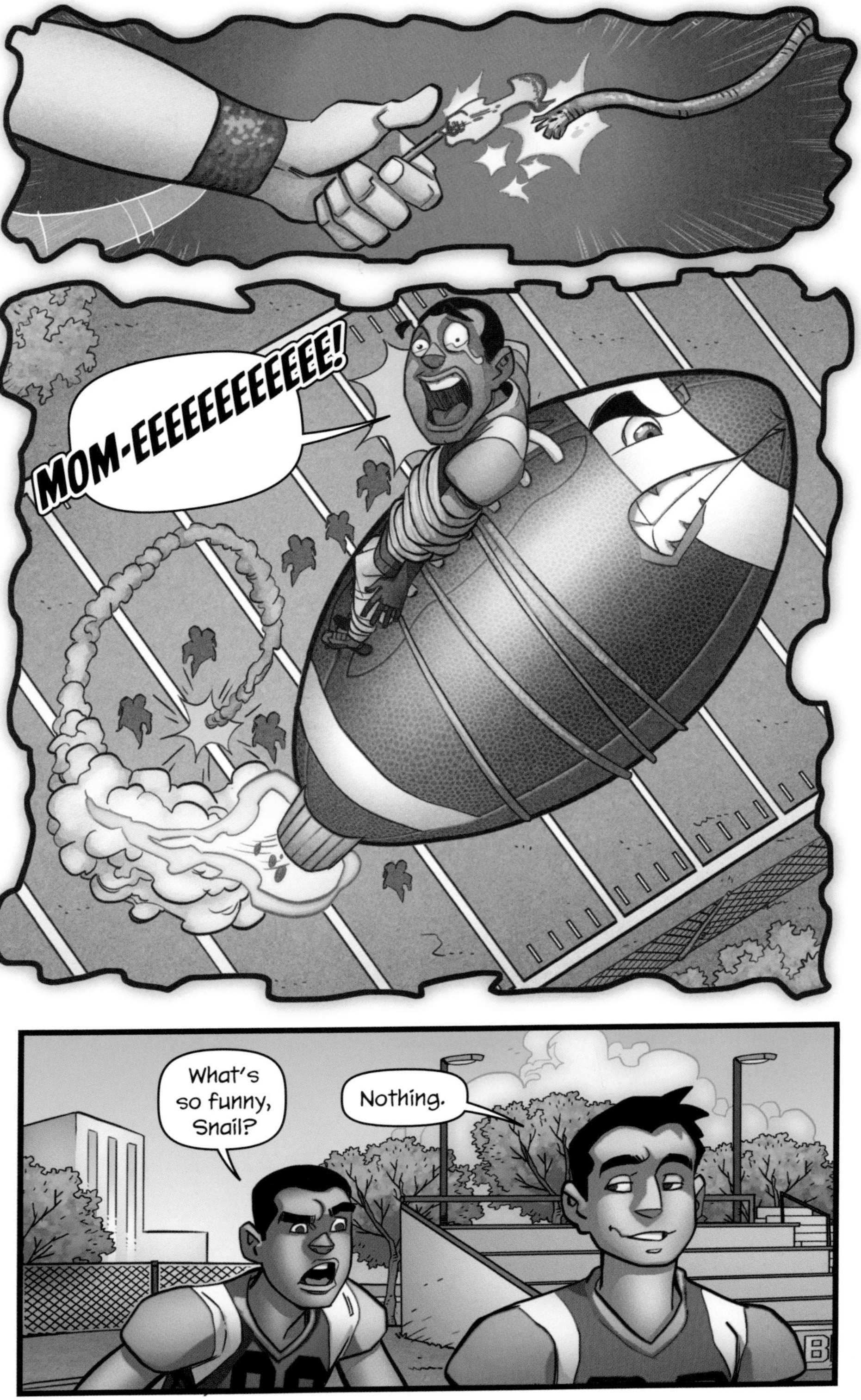
MOM-EEEEEEEEEEEE!
What's so funny, Snail?
Nothing.

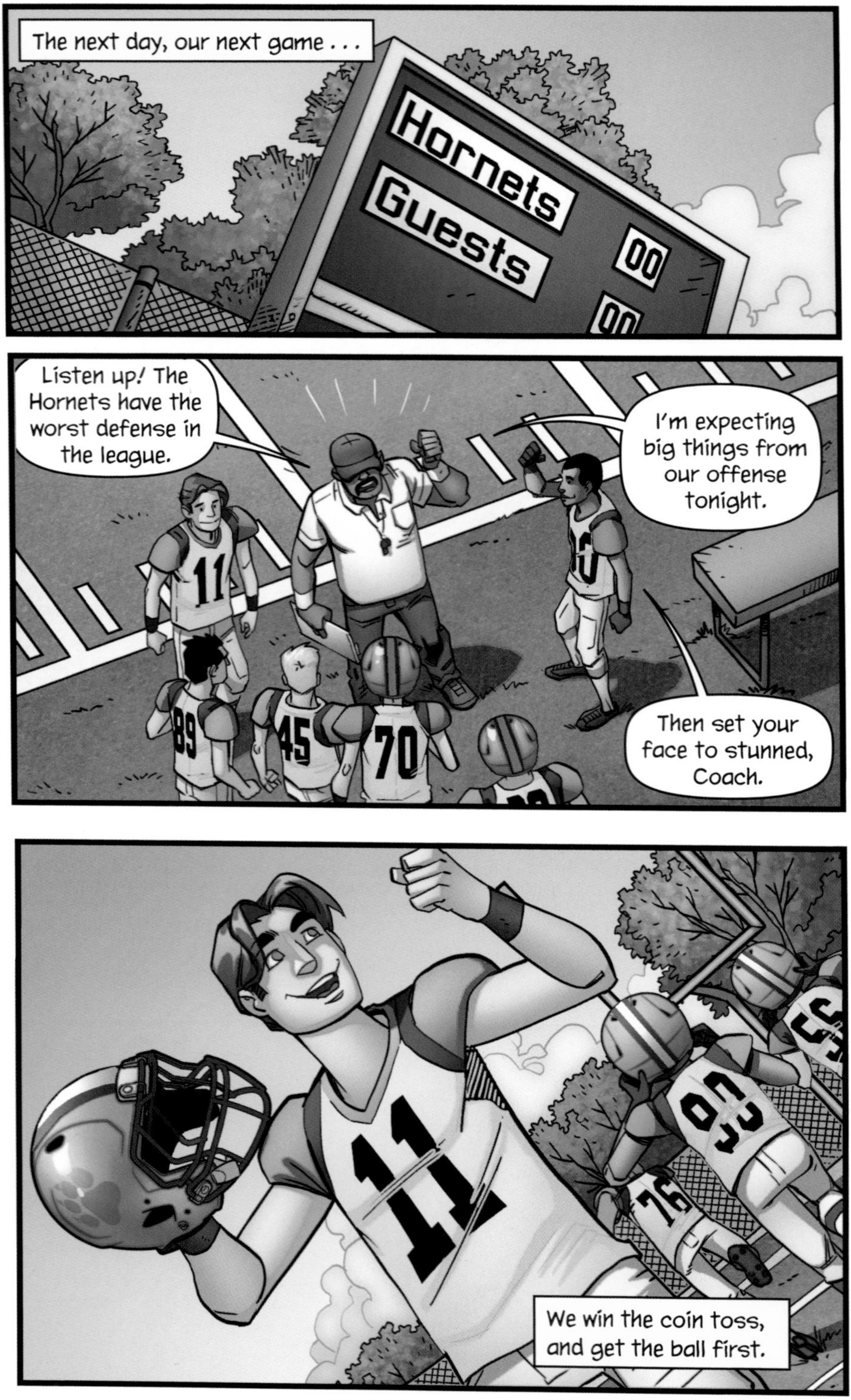
The next day, our next game . . .
Hornets
Guests
00
00
Listen up! The Hornets have the worst defense in the league.
I'm expecting big things from our offense tonight.
Then set your face to stunned, Coach.
We win the coin toss, and get the ball first.

I take my usual position, of course.

We strike early . . .

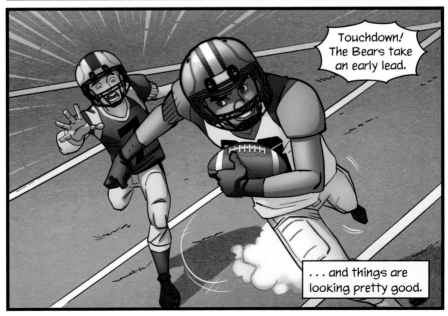

Touchdown! The Bears take an early lead.

. . . and things are looking pretty good.

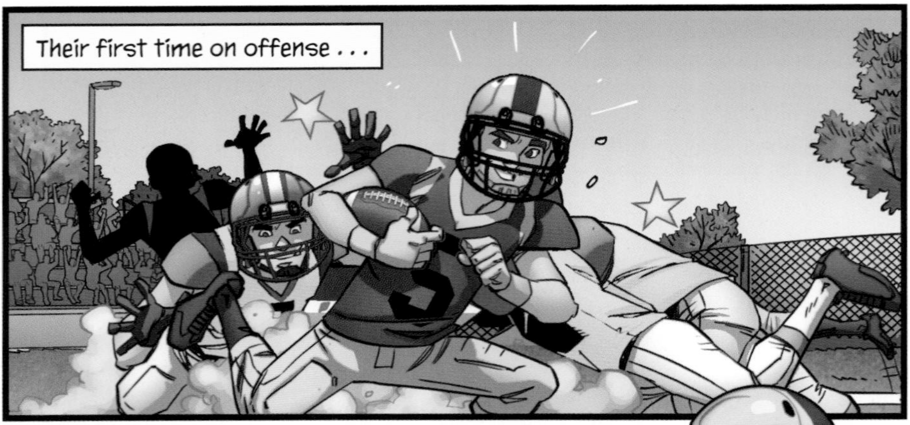
Their first time on offense . . .

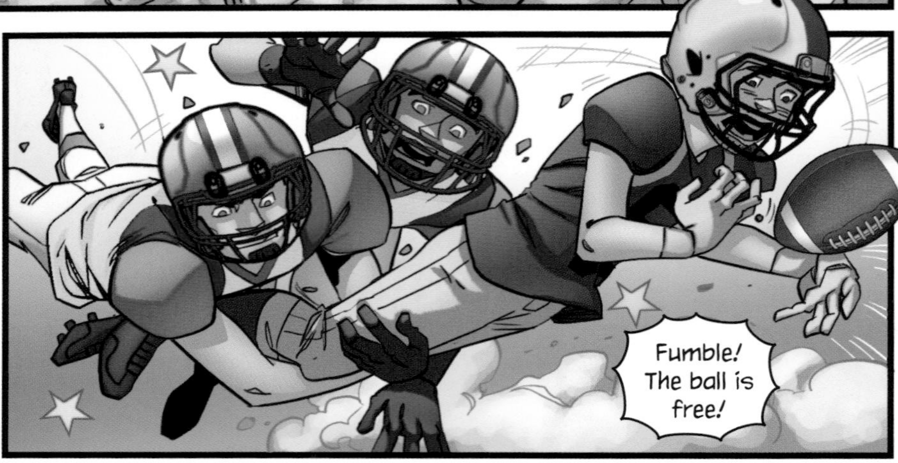
Fumble! The ball is free!

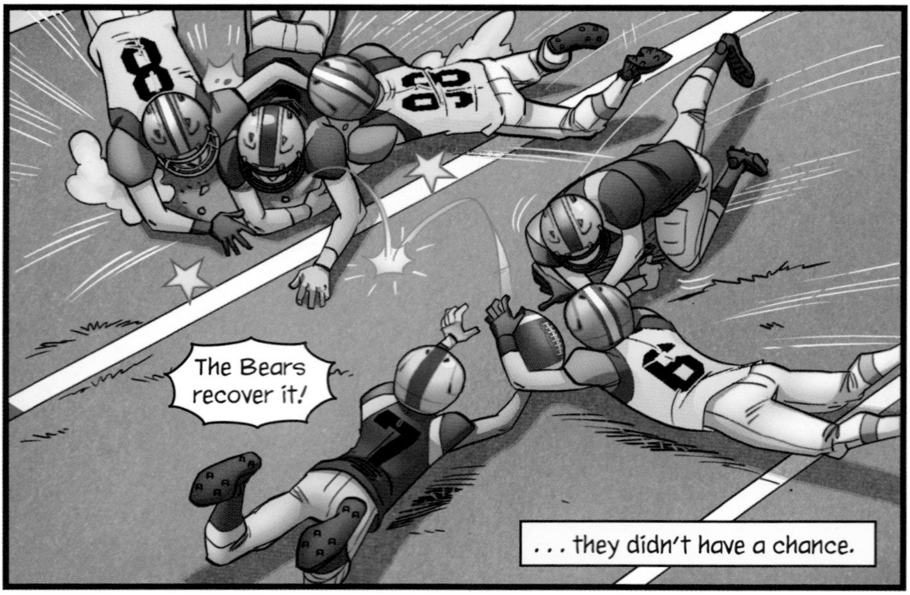
The Bears recover it!
. . . they didn't have a chance.

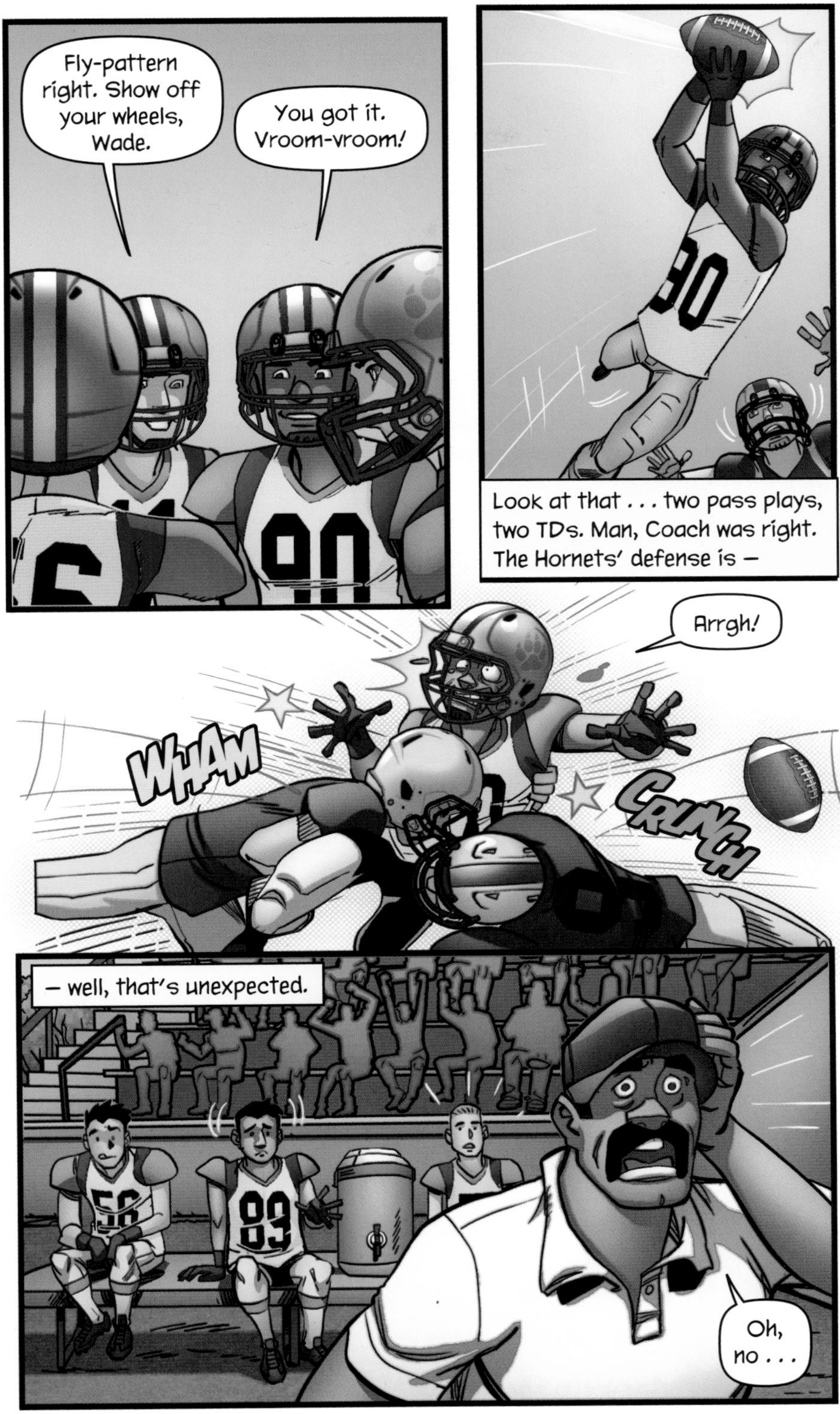
Fly-pattern right. Show off your wheels, Wade.
You got it. Vroom-vroom!
Look at that . . . two pass plays, two TDs. Man, Coach was right. The Hornets' defense is —
Arrgh!
WHAM
CRUNCH
— well, that's unexpected.
Oh, no . . .

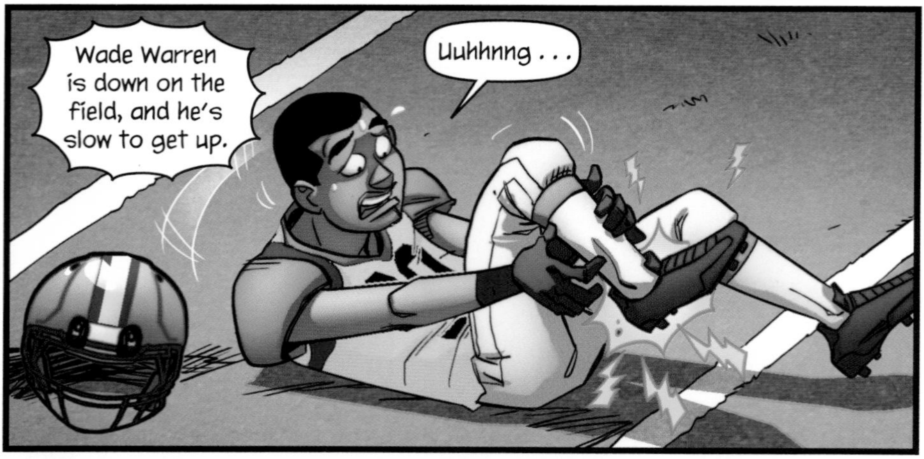
Wade Warren is down on the field, and he's slow to get up.
Uuhhnng . . .

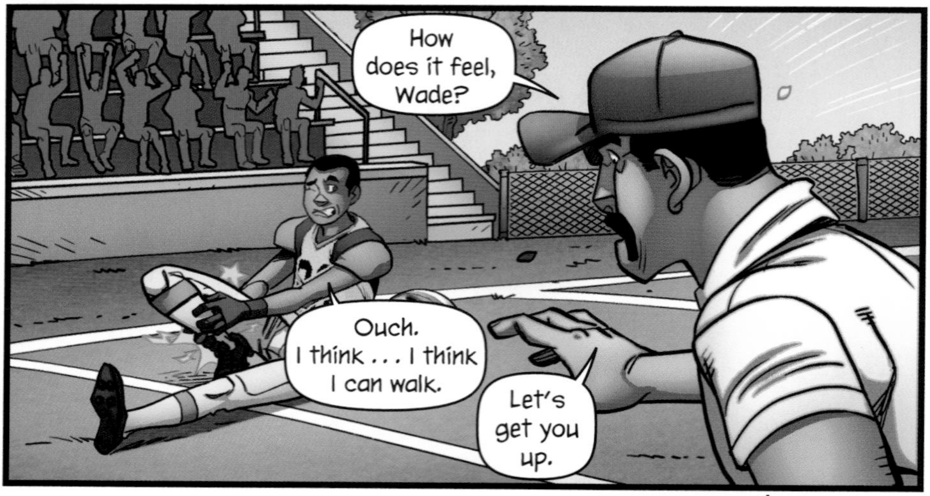
How does it feel, Wade?
Ouch. I think . . . I think I can walk.
Let's get you up.

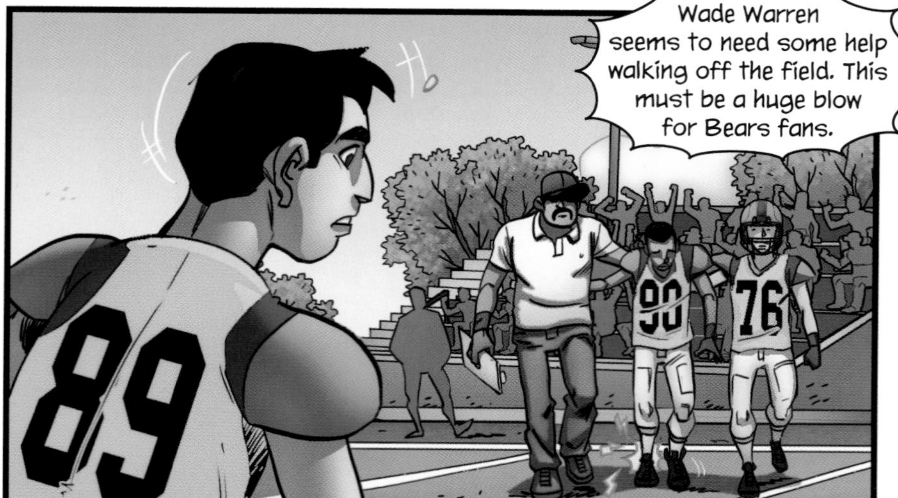
Wade Warren seems to need some help walking off the field. This must be a huge blow for Bears fans.
90
76
89

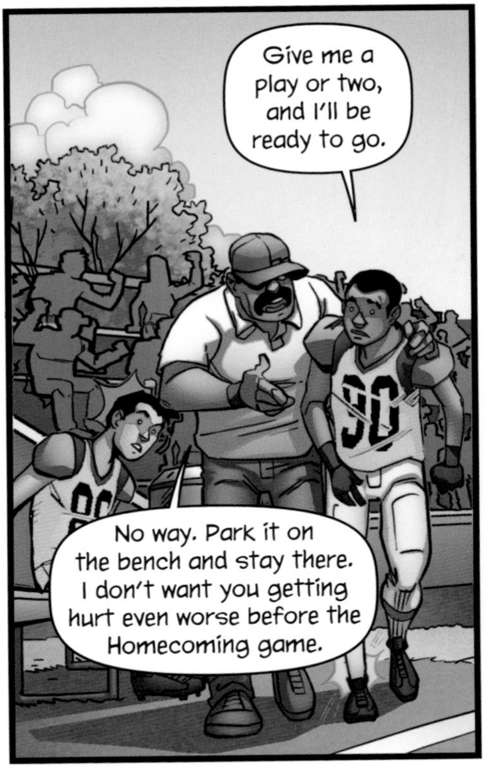
Give me a play or two, and I'll be ready to go.
No way. Park it on the bench and stay there. I don't want you getting hurt even worse before the Homecoming game.

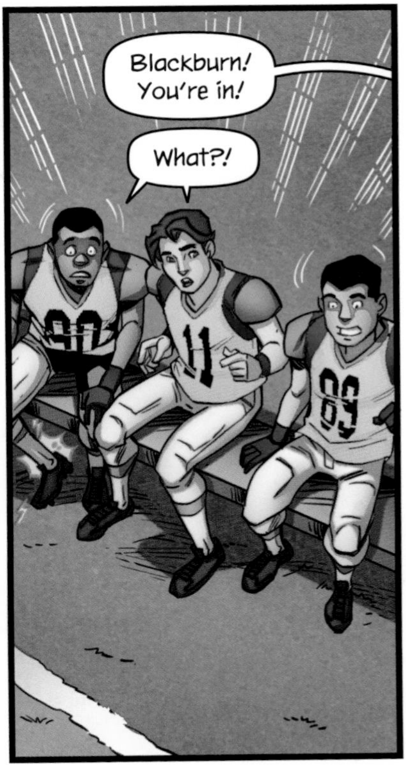
Blackburn! You're in!
What?!

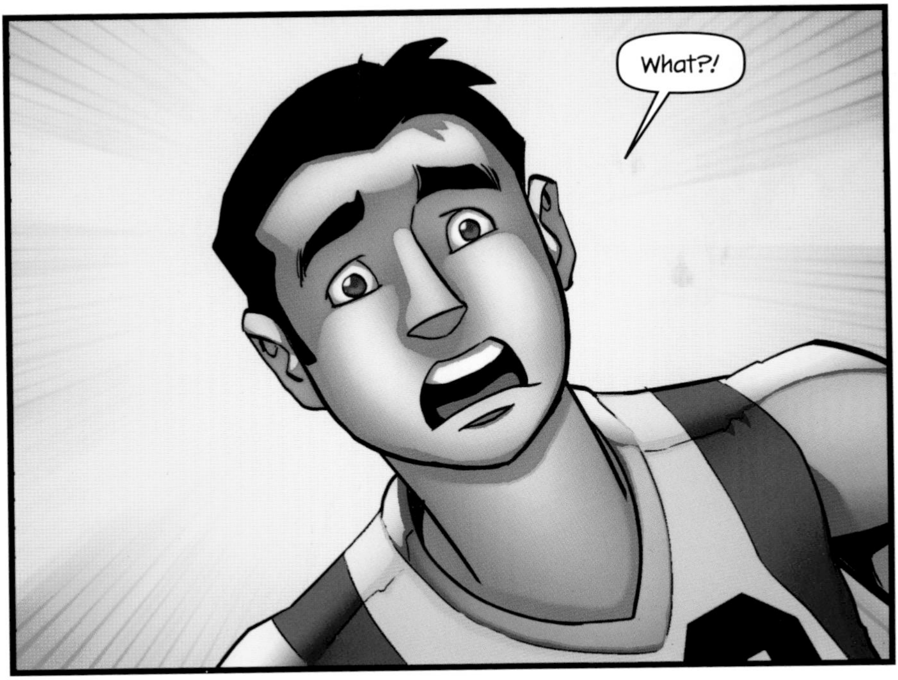
What?!

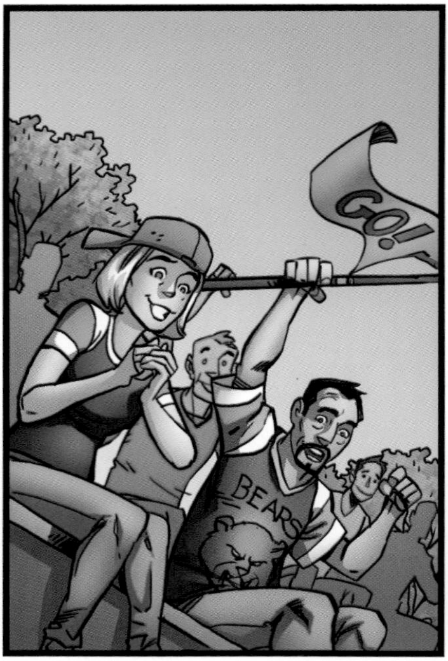
GO!
BEARS

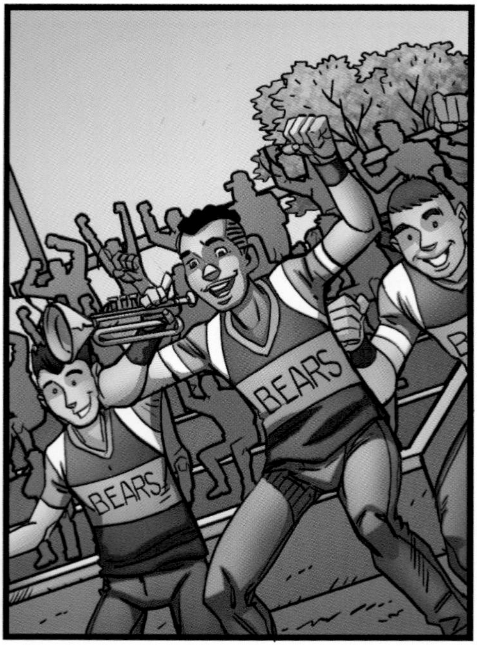
BEARS
BEARS

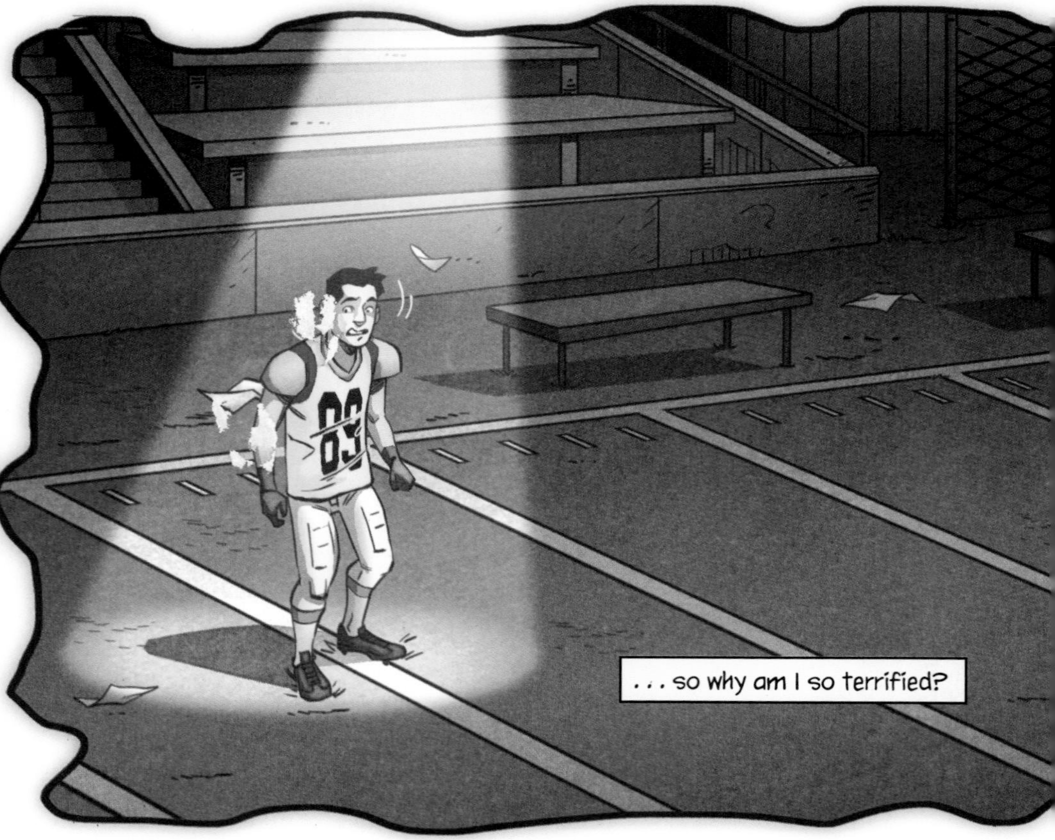
. . . so why am I so terrified?

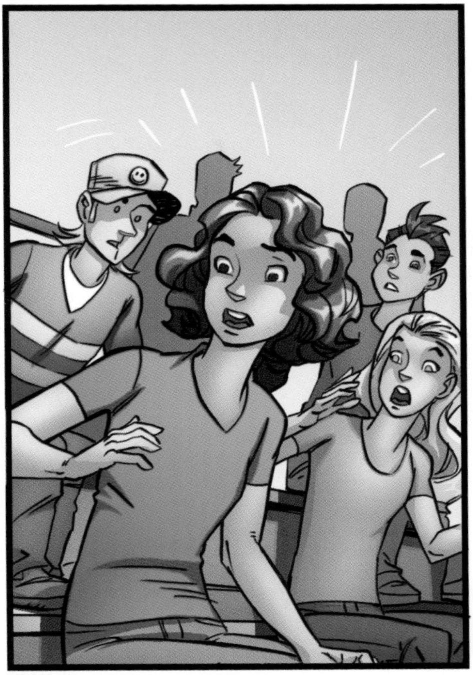

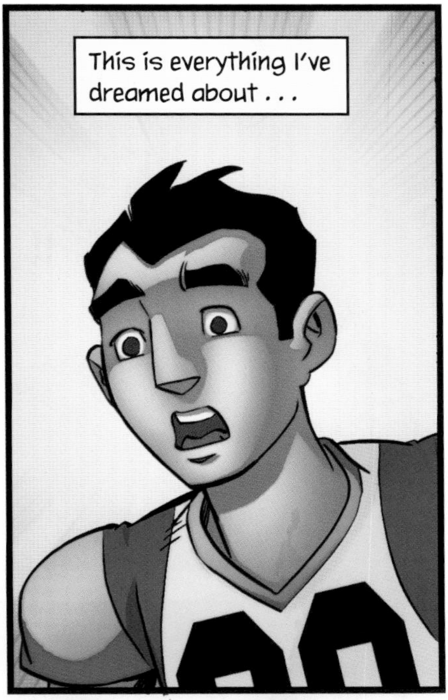
This is everything I've dreamed about . . .

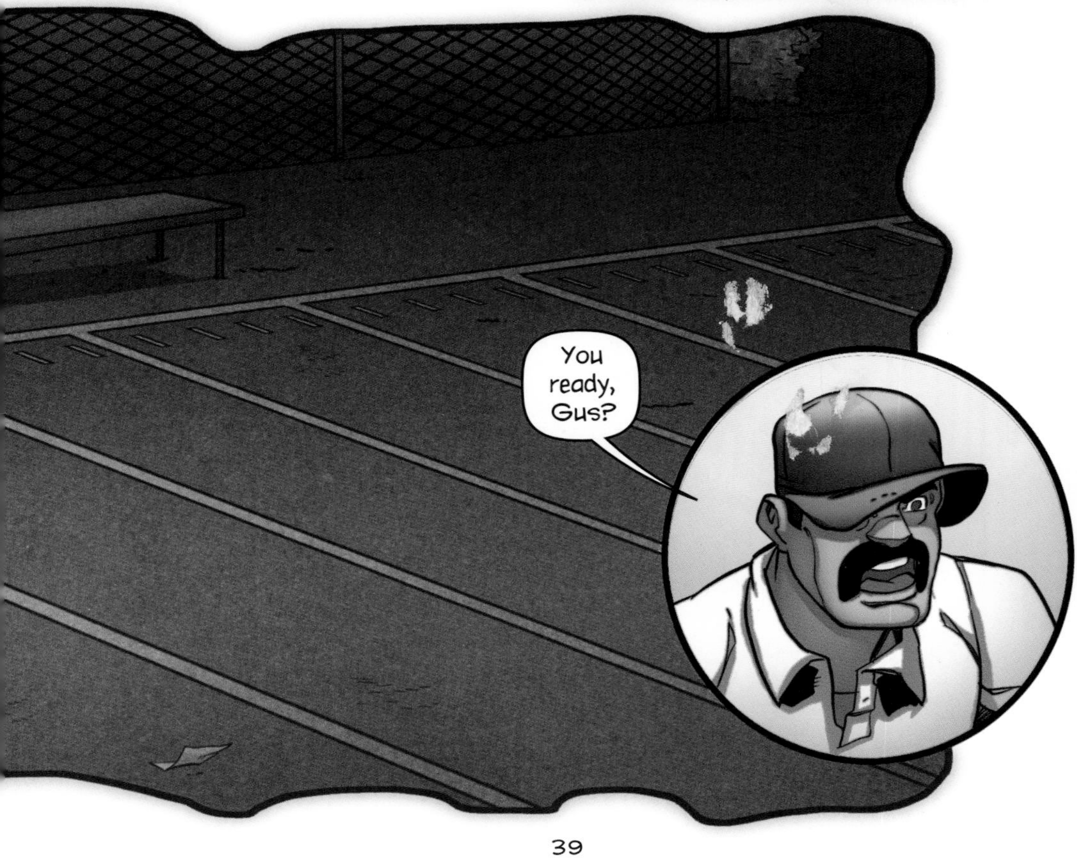
You ready, Gus?

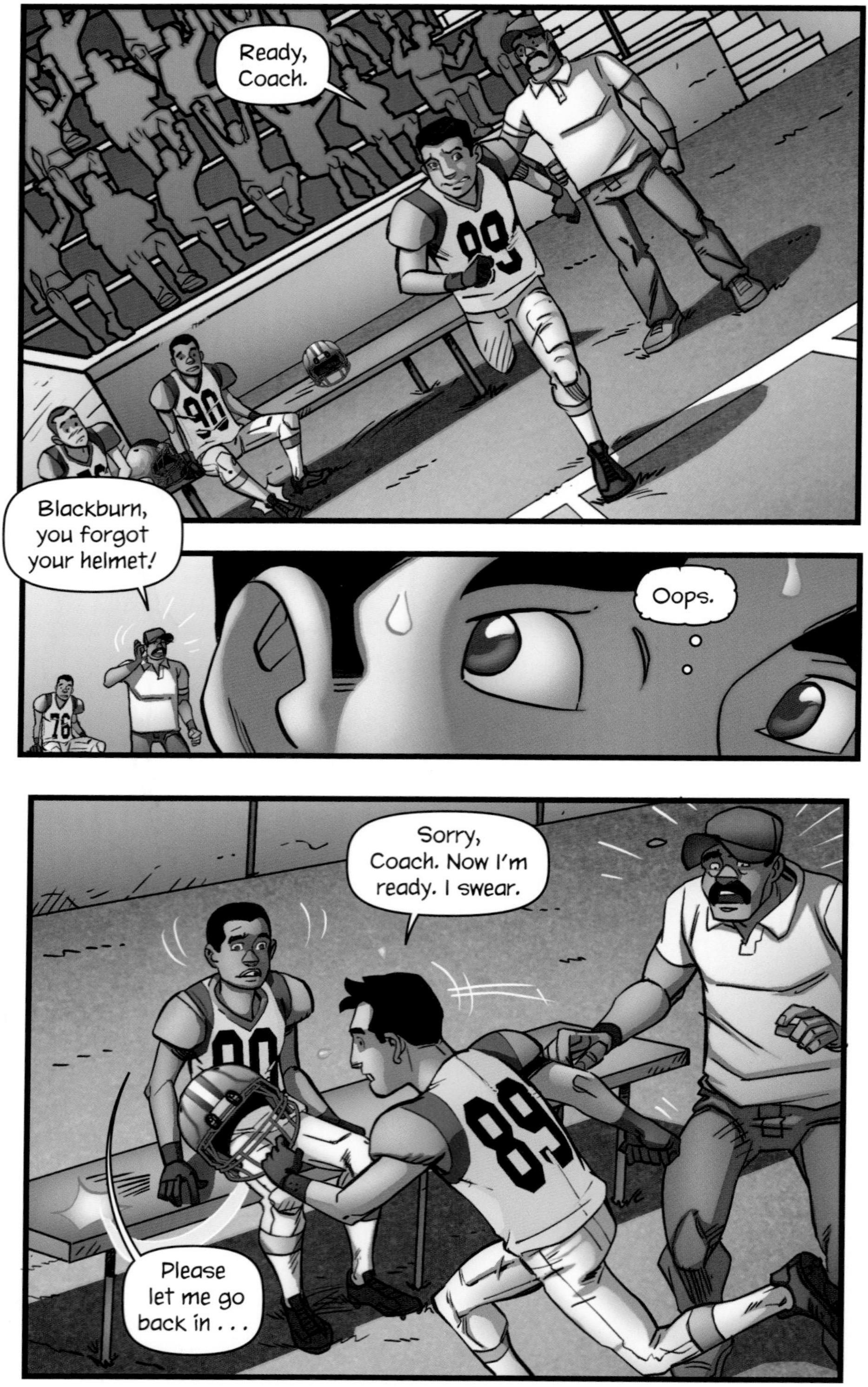
Ready, Coach.
Blackburn, you forgot your helmet!
Oops.
Sorry, Coach. Now I'm ready. I swear.
Please let me go back in . . .

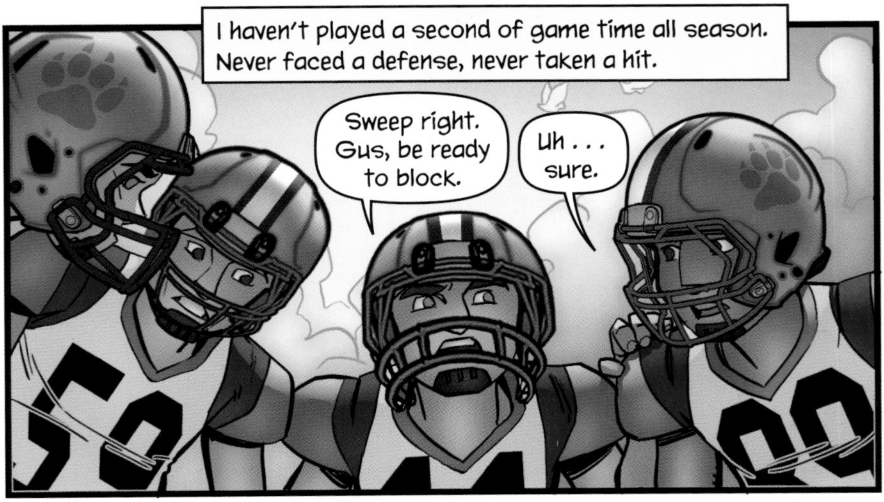
I haven't played a second of game time all season. Never faced a defense, never taken a hit.
Sweep right. Gus, be ready to block.
Uh . . . sure.

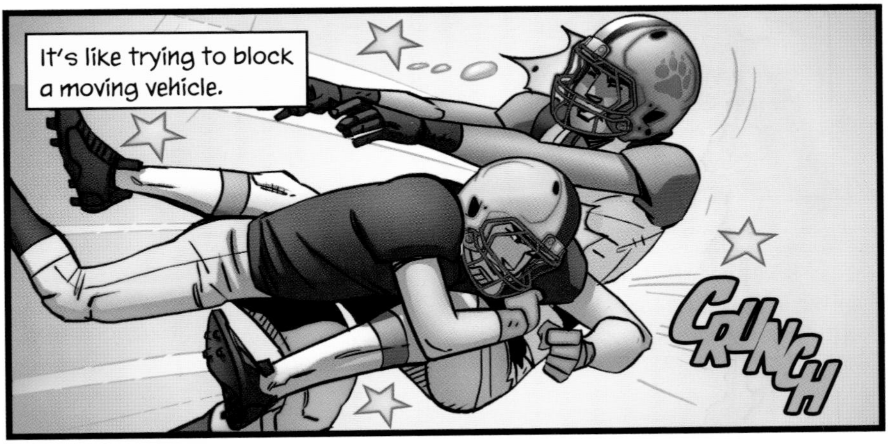
It's like trying to block a moving vehicle.
CRUNCH

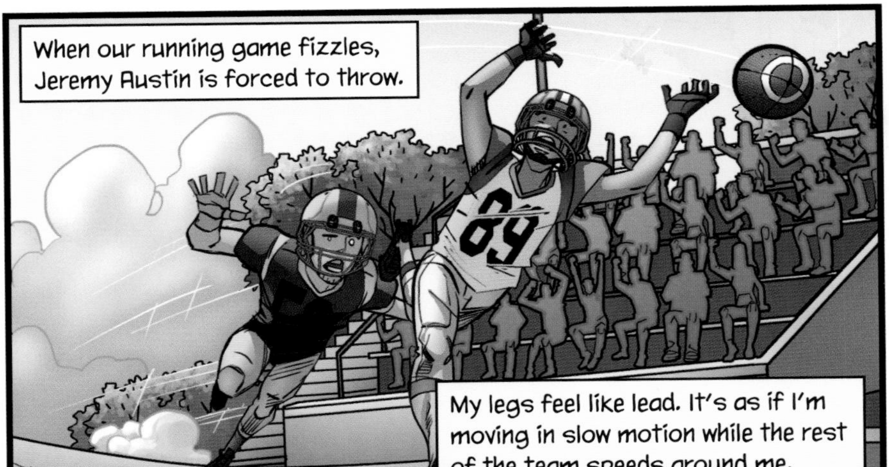
When our running game fizzles, Jeremy Austin is forced to throw.
My legs feel like lead. It's as if I'm moving in slow motion while the rest of the team speeds around me.

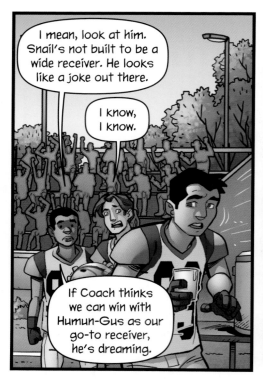

I mean, look at him. Snail's not built to be a wide receiver. He looks like a joke out there.

I know, I know.

If Coach thinks we can win with Humun-Gus as our go-to receiver, he's dreaming.

Jeremy adjusts for my speed (or my lack of it), but that only makes things worse.

Interception, Hornets!

They have the worst defense in the league, and I hand them a TD on a silver platter.

Another Hornets touchdown!

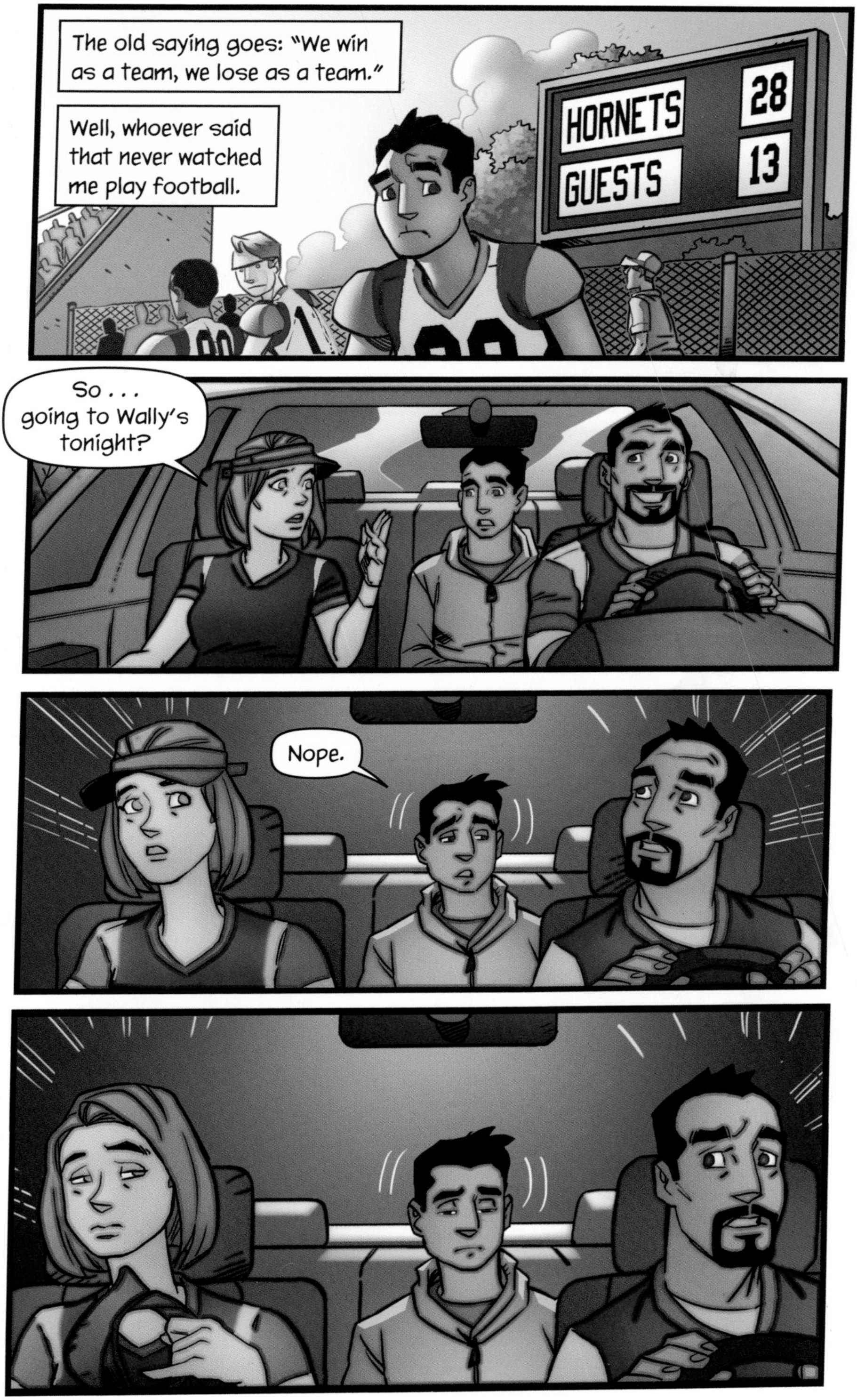
The old saying goes: "We win as a team, we lose as a team."
Well, whoever said that never watched me play football.
HORNETS 28
GUESTS 13
So . . . going to Wally's tonight?
Nope.

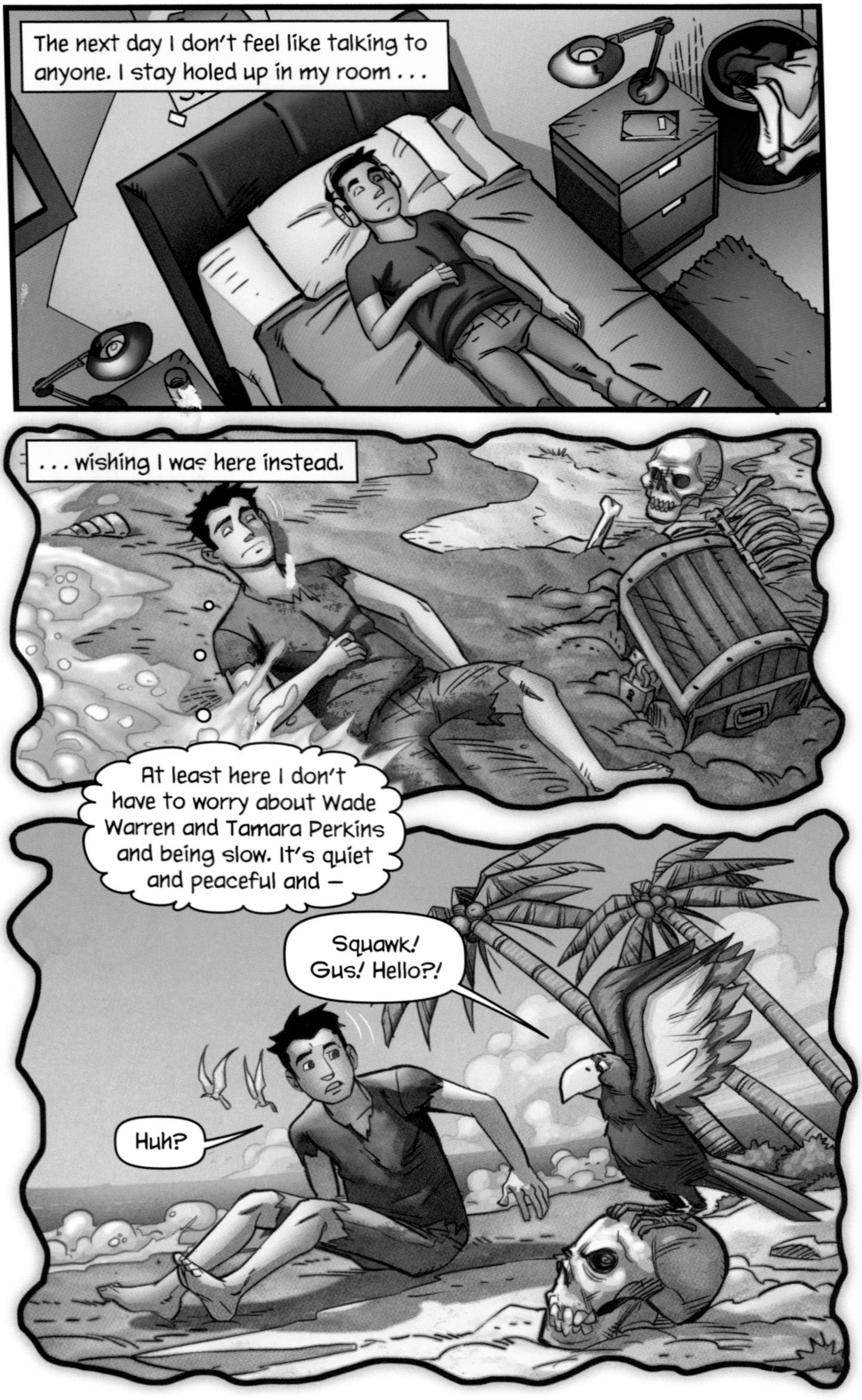

The next day I don't feel like talking to anyone. I stay holed up in my room . . .
. . . wishing I was here instead.
At least here I don't have to worry about Wade Warren and Tamara Perkins and being slow. It's quiet and peaceful and —
Squawk! Gus! Hello?!
Huh?

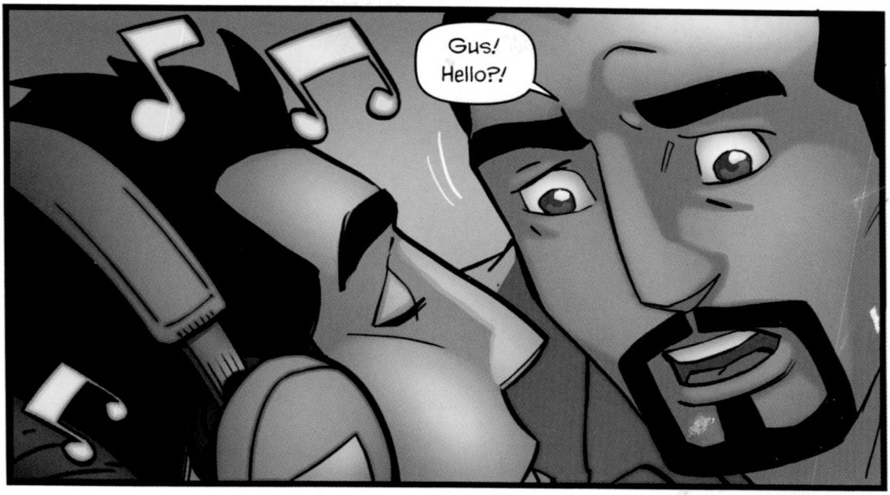
Gus!
Hello?!

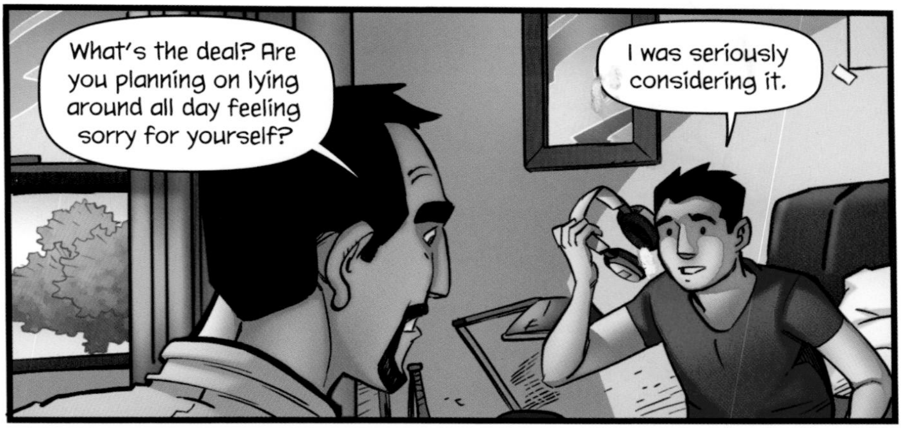
What's the deal? Are you planning on lying around all day feeling sorry for yourself?
I was seriously considering it.

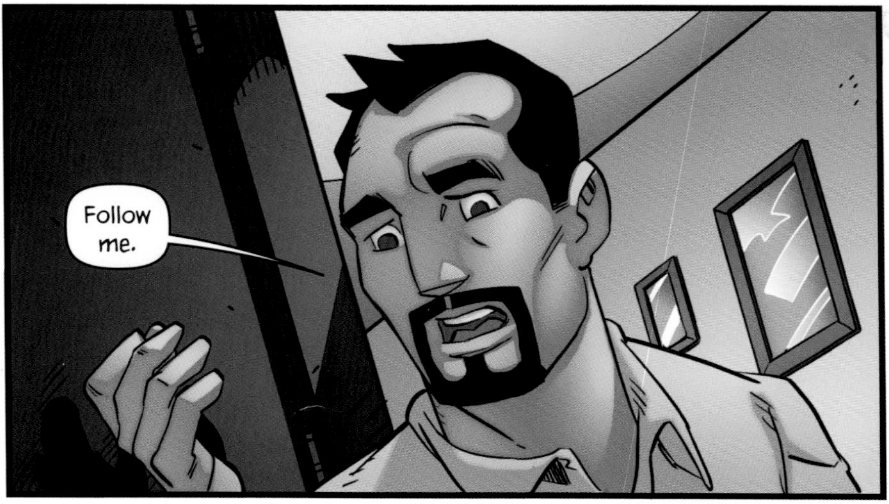
Follow me.

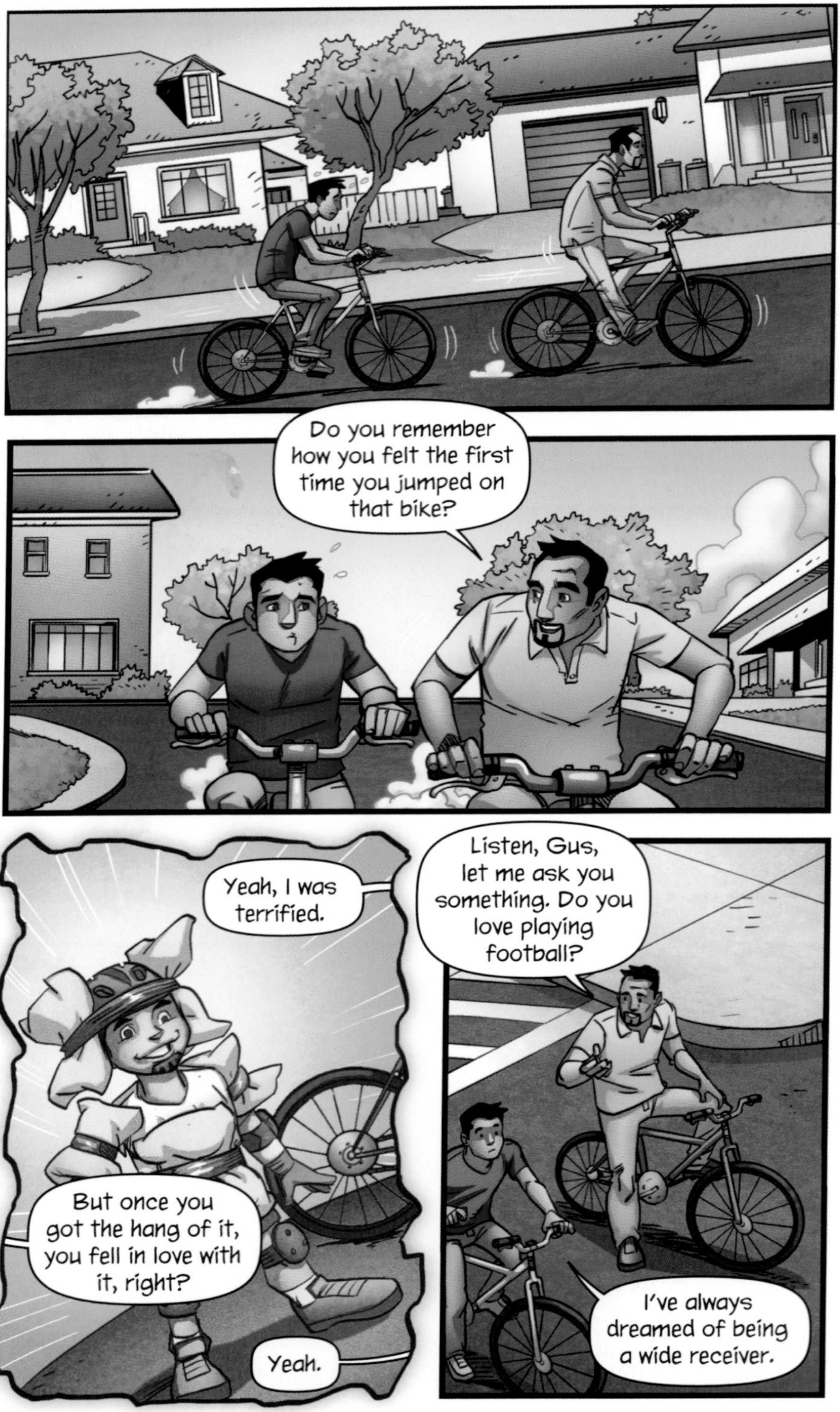
Do you remember how you felt the first time you jumped on that bike?
Yeah, I was terrified.
But once you got the hang of it, you fell in love with it, right?
Yeah.
Listen, Gus, let me ask you something. Do you love playing football?
I've always dreamed of being a wide receiver.

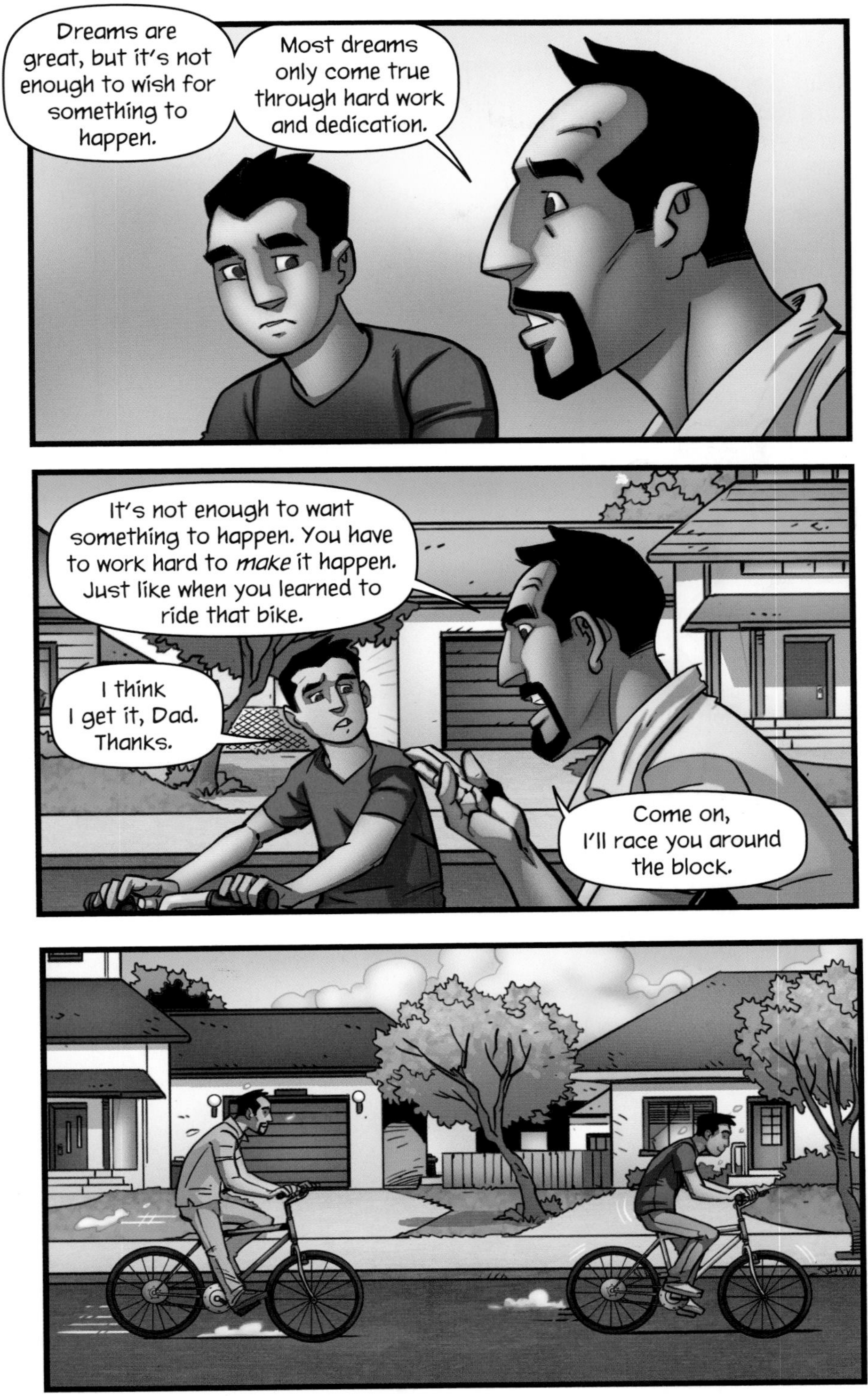
Dreams are great, but it's not enough to wish for something to happen.
Most dreams only come true through hard work and dedication.
It's not enough to want something to happen. You have to work hard to *make* it happen. Just like when you learned to ride that bike.
I think I get it, Dad. Thanks.
Come on, I'll race you around the block.

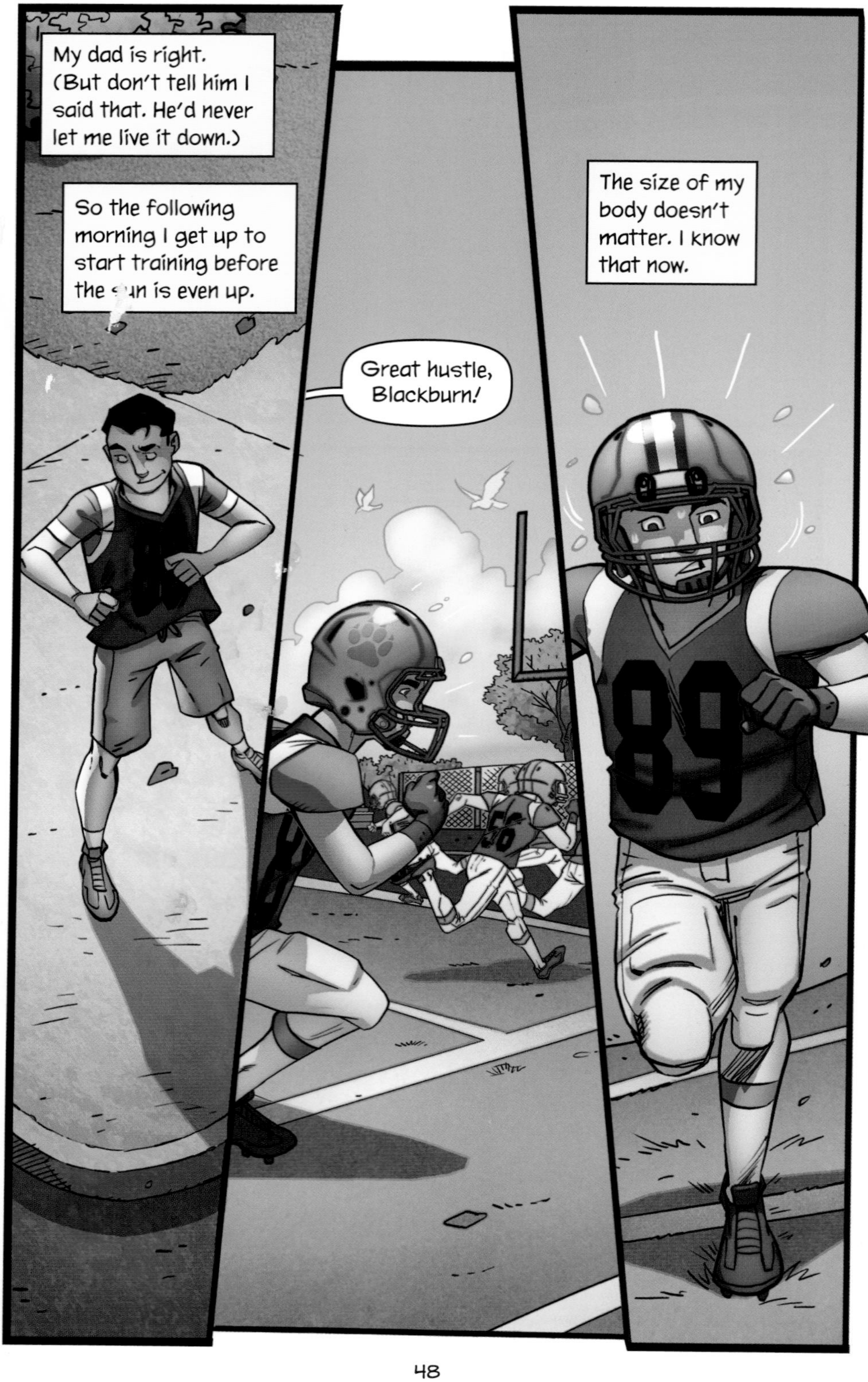
My dad is right. (But don't tell him I said that. He'd never let me live it down.)
So the following morning I get up to start training before the sun is even up.
Great hustle, Blackburn!
The size of my body doesn't matter. I know that now.
89

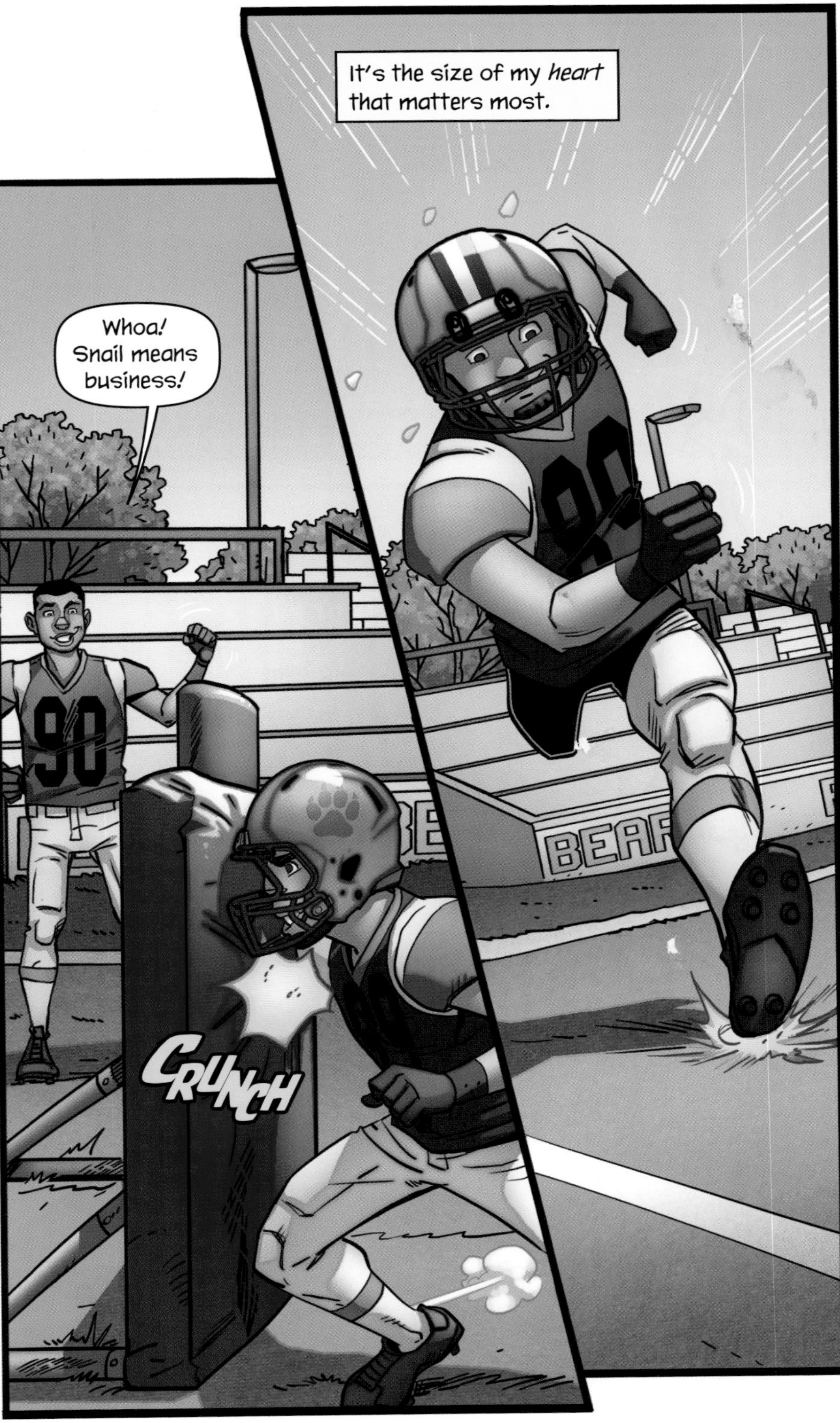
It's the size of my *heart* that matters most.
Whoa! Snail means business!
CRUNCH
BEAR

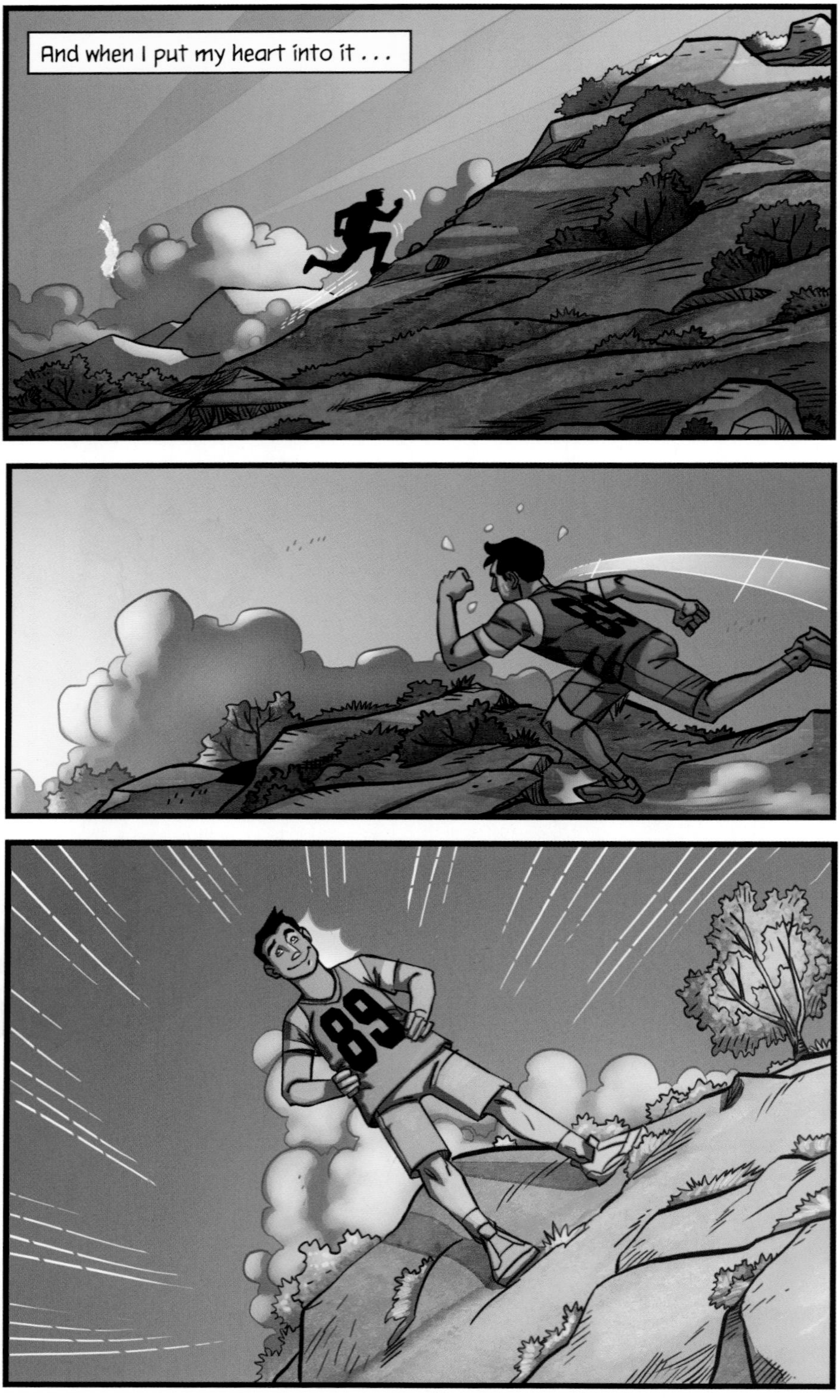
And when I put my heart into it . . .

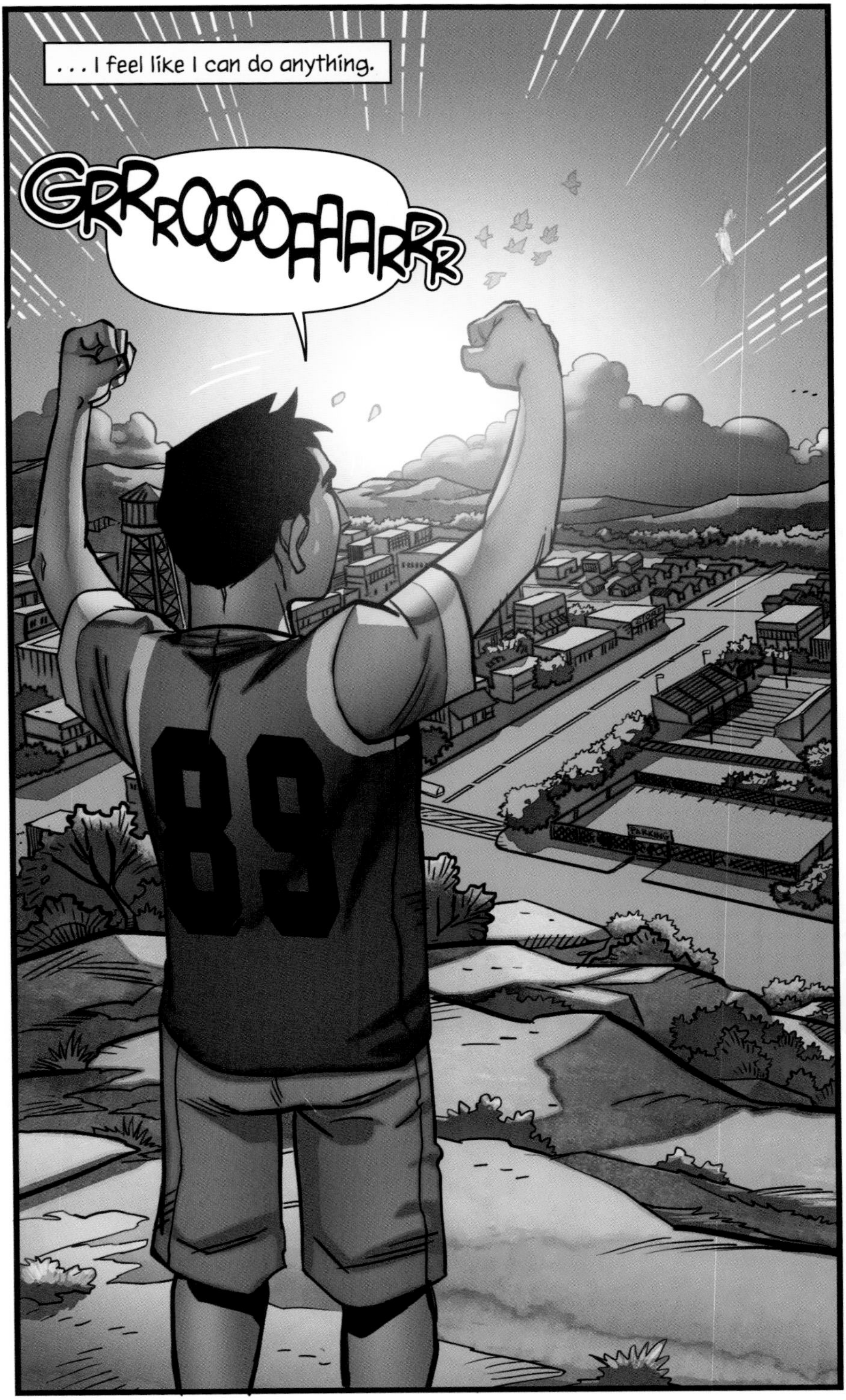
. . . I feel like I can do anything.
GRRRROOOOAAARRRR
PARKING

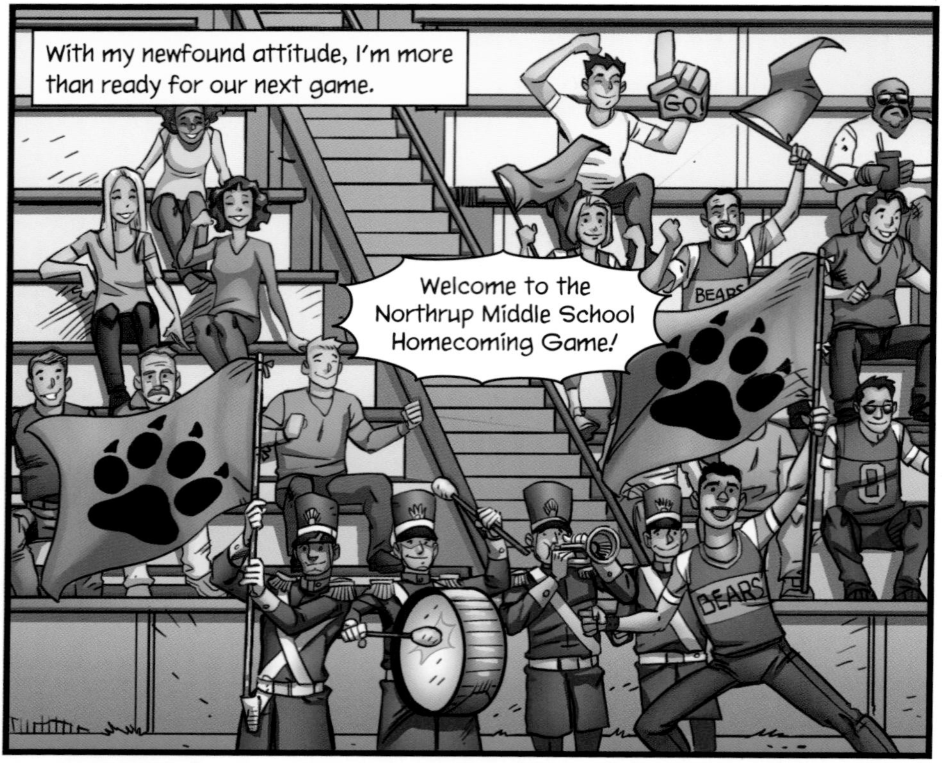

With my newfound attitude, I'm more than ready for our next game.
Welcome to the Northrup Middle School Homecoming Game!
GO!
BEARS
BEARS

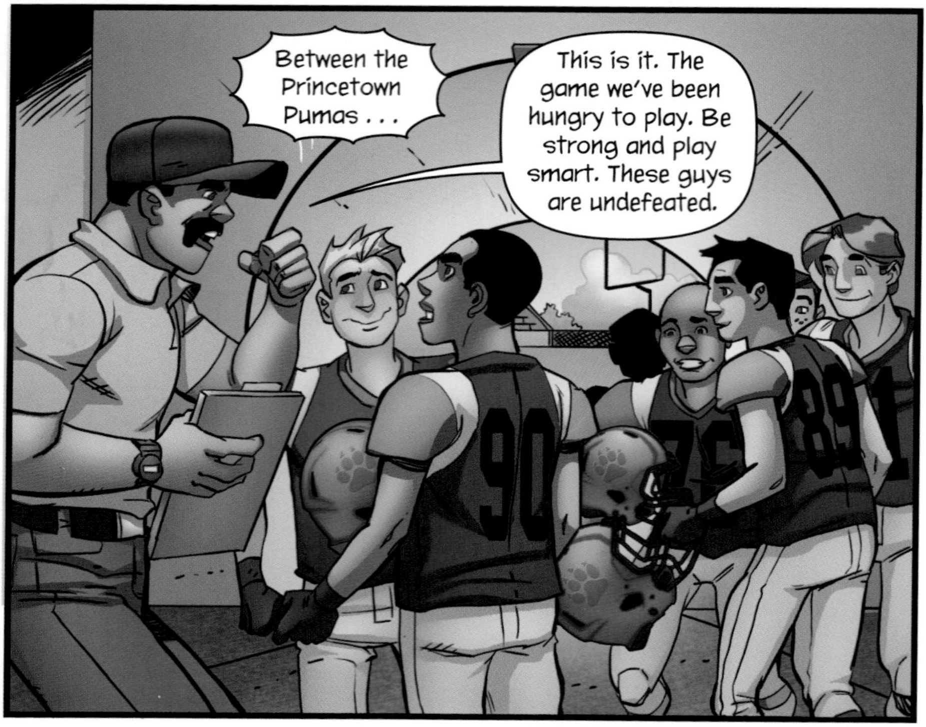

Between the Princetown Pumas . . .
This is it. The game we've been hungry to play. Be strong and play smart. These guys are undefeated.

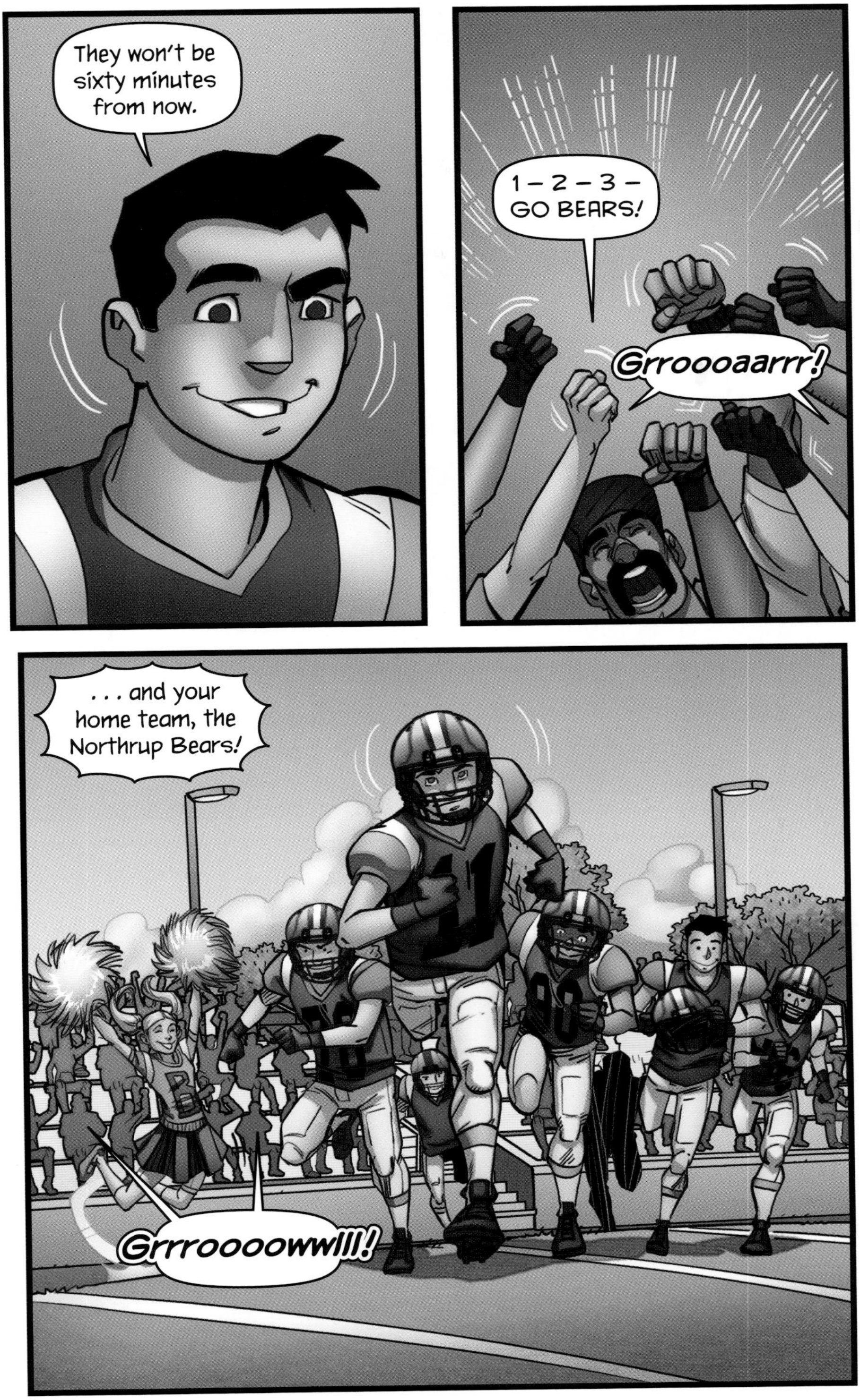
They won't be sixty minutes from now.
1 – 2 – 3 – GO BEARS!
Grroooaarrr!
. . . and your home team, the Northrup Bears!
Grrroooowwlll!

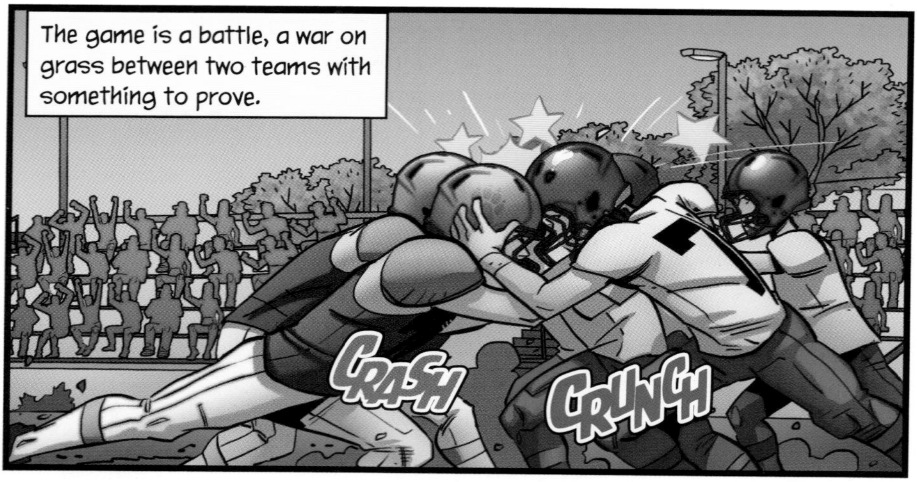
The game is a battle, a war on grass between two teams with something to prove.
CRASH
CRUNCH

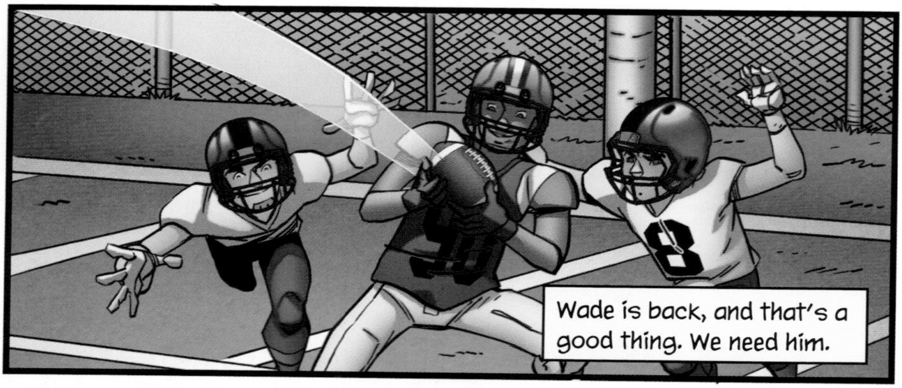
Wade is back, and that's a good thing. We need him.

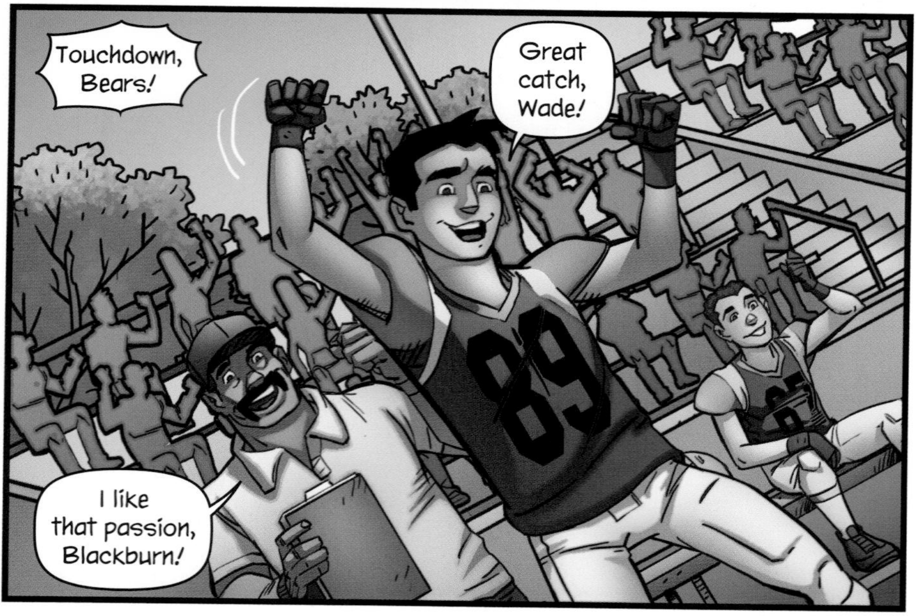
Touchdown, Bears!
Great catch, Wade!
I like that passion, Blackburn!

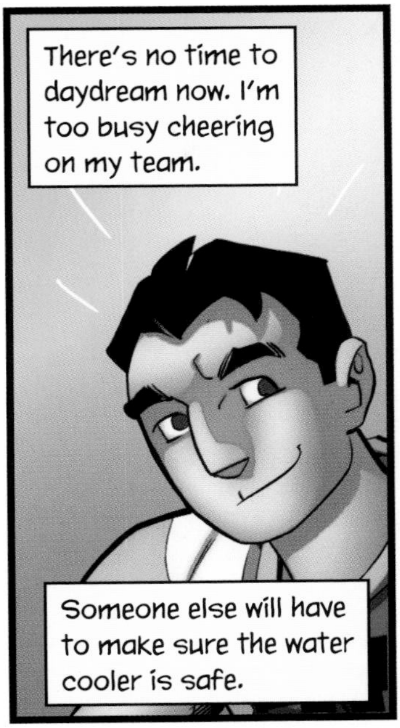
There's no time to daydream now. I'm too busy cheering on my team.
Someone else will have to make sure the water cooler is safe.

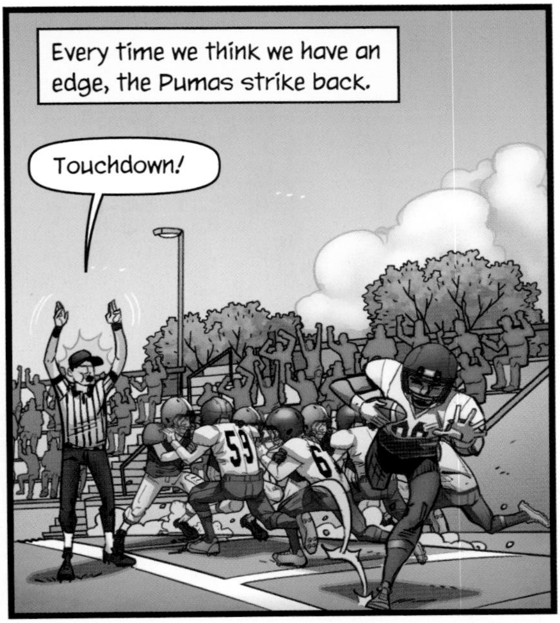
Every time we think we have an edge, the Pumas strike back.
Touchdown!

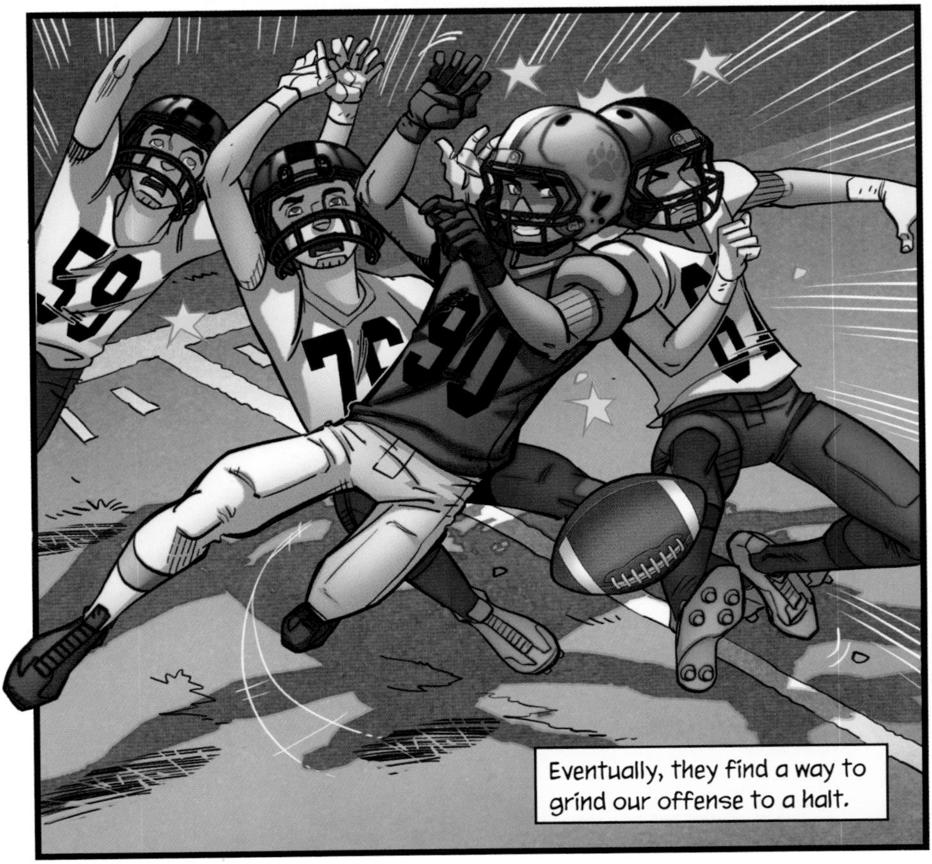
Eventually, they find a way to grind our offense to a halt.

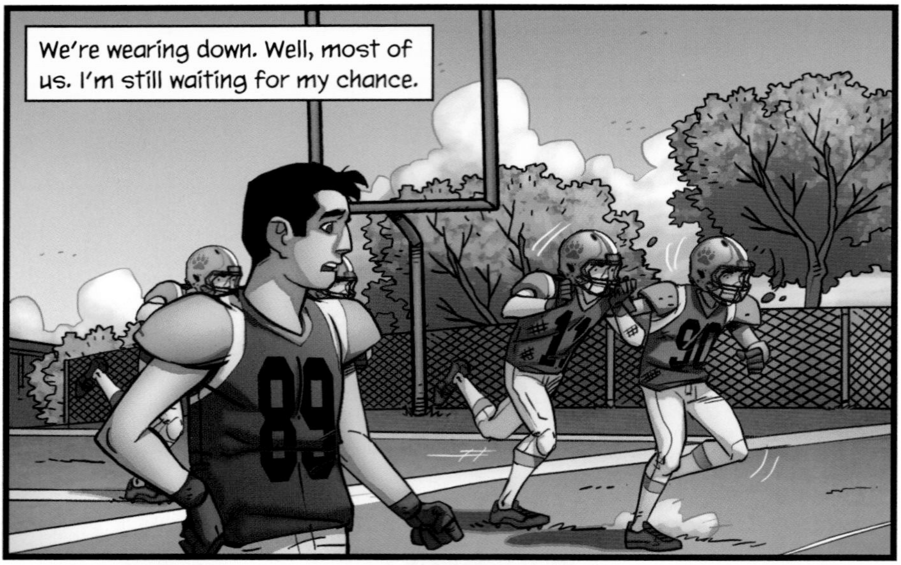
We're wearing down. Well, most of us. I'm still waiting for my chance.
89
11
90

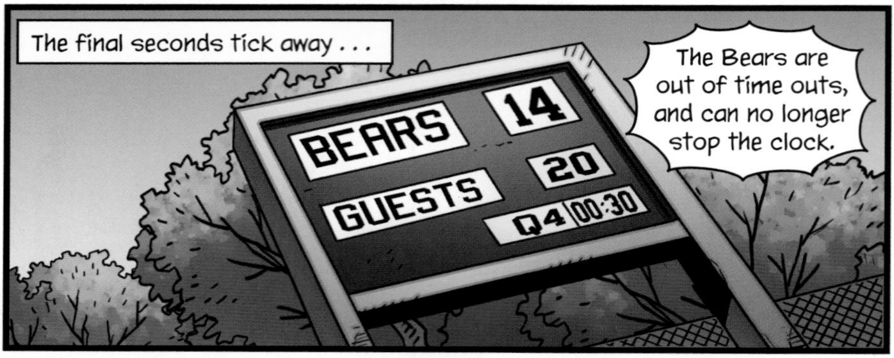
The final seconds tick away . . .
BEARS 14
GUESTS 20
Q4 00:30
The Bears are out of time outs, and can no longer stop the clock.

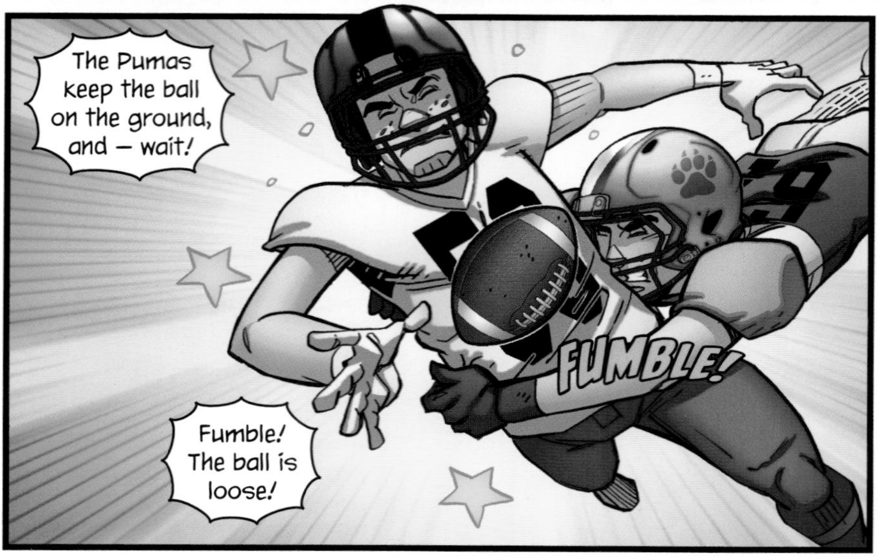
The Pumas keep the ball on the ground, and — wait!
FUMBLE!
Fumble! The ball is loose!

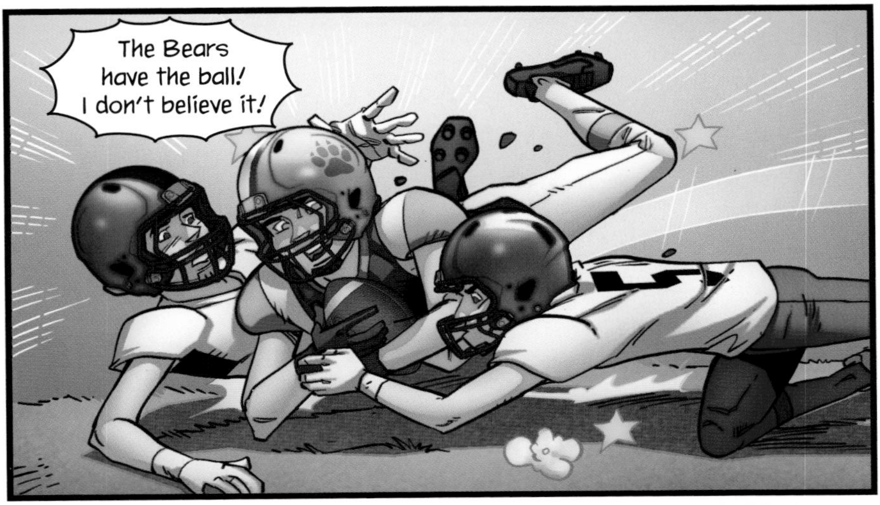
The Bears have the ball! I don't believe it!

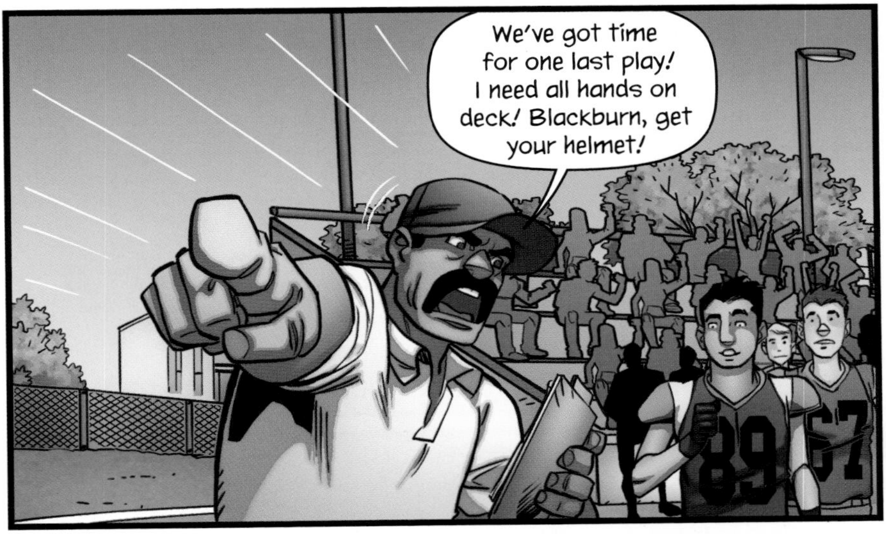
We've got time for one last play! I need all hands on deck! Blackburn, get your helmet!

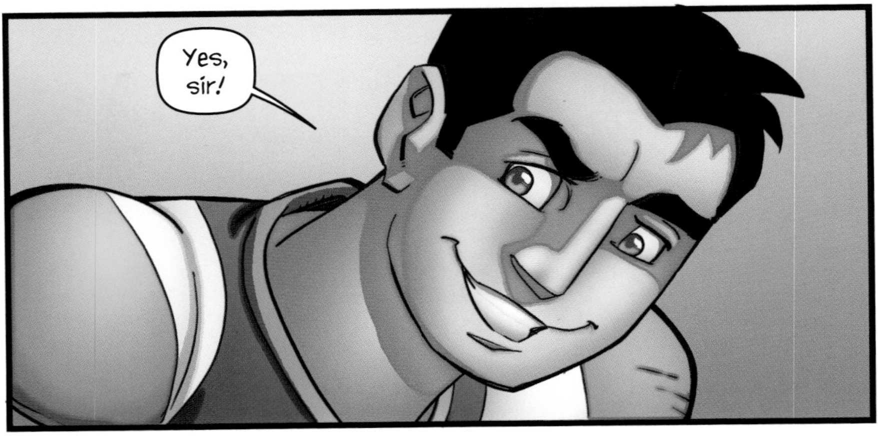
Yes, sir!

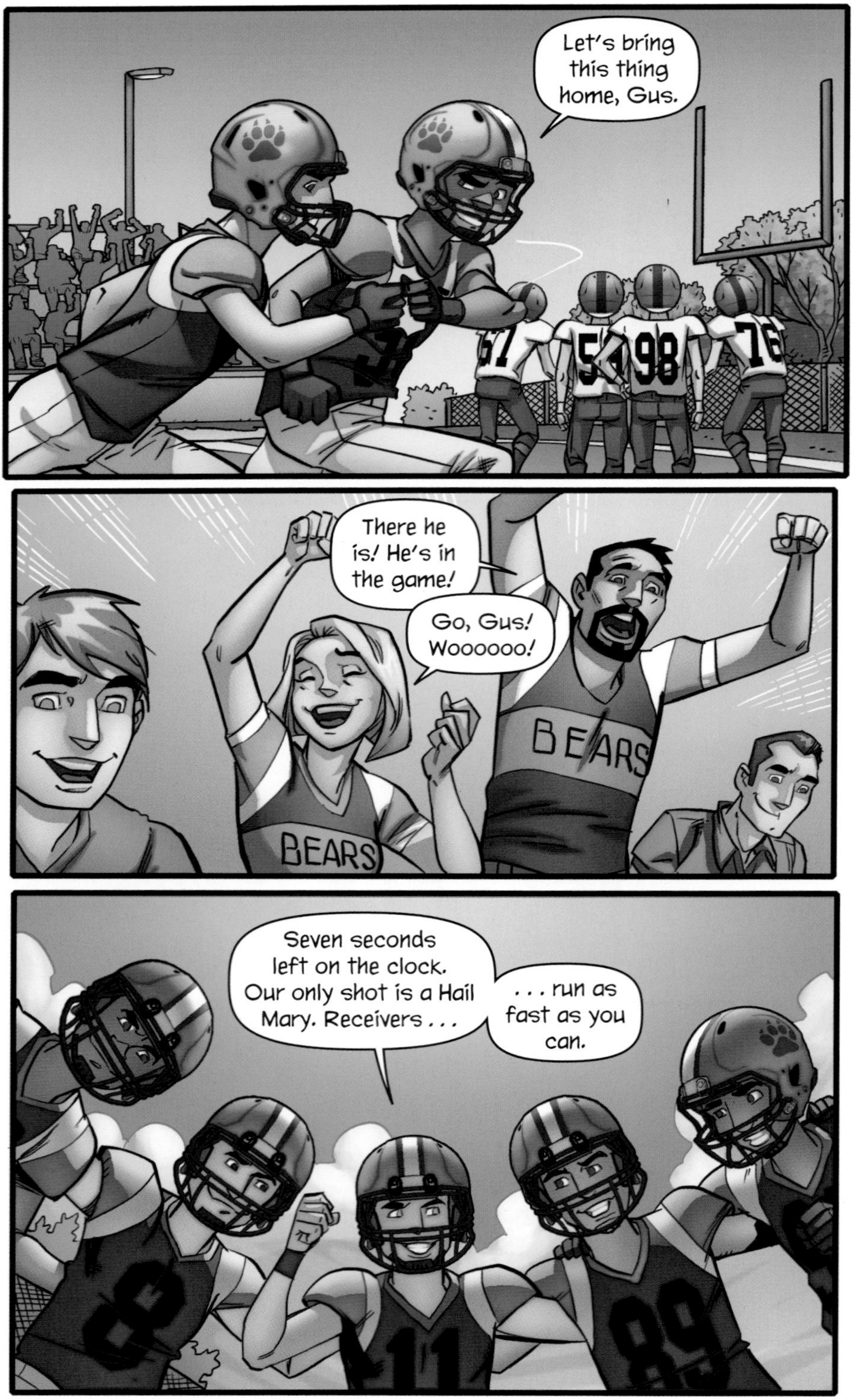
Let's bring this thing home, Gus.
There he is! He's in the game!
Go, Gus! Woooooo!
BEARS
BEARS
Seven seconds left on the clock. Our only shot is a Hail Mary. Receivers . . .
. . . run as fast as you can.

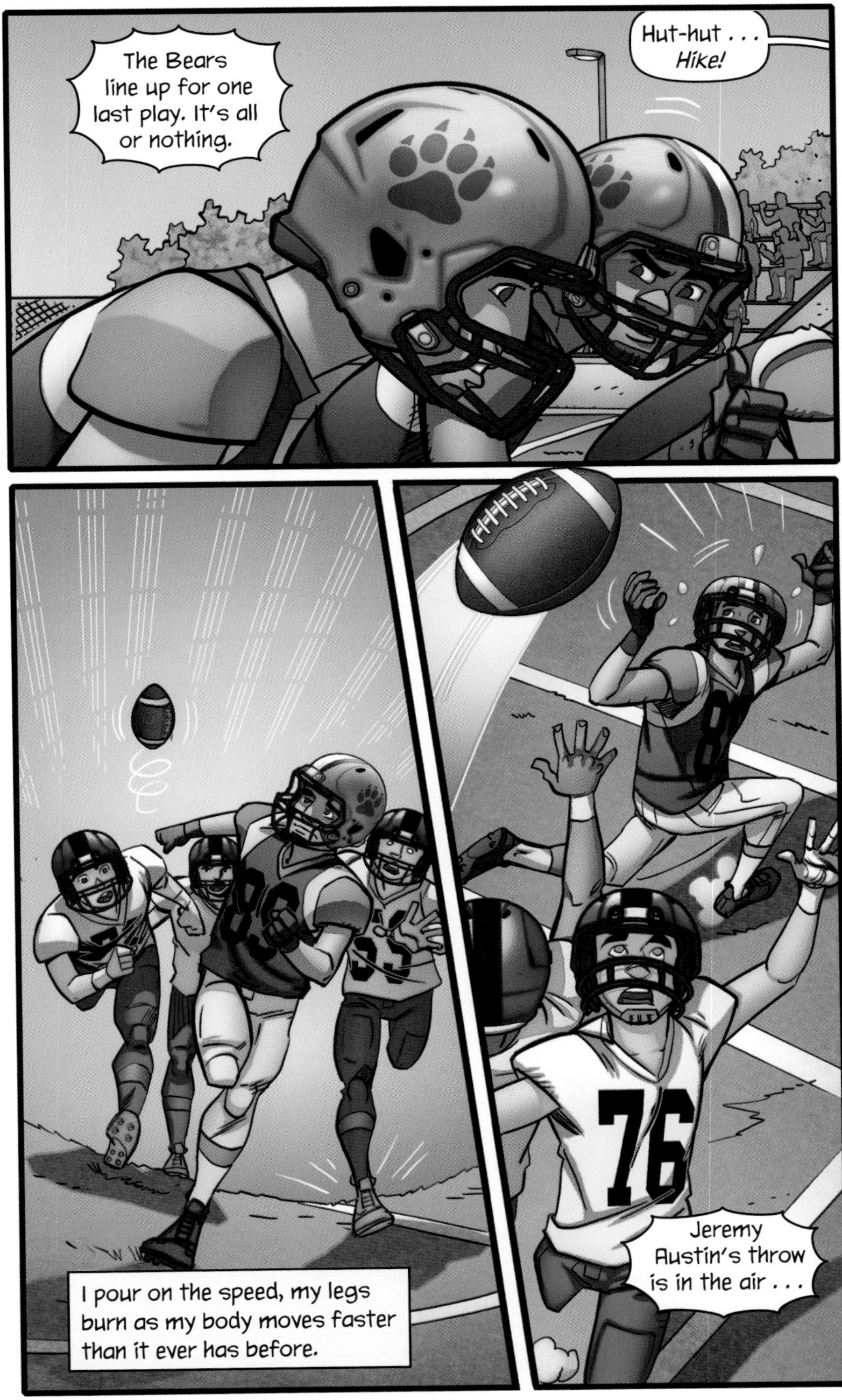
The Bears line up for one last play. It's all or nothing.
Hut-hut . . . *Hike!*
I pour on the speed, my legs burn as my body moves faster than it ever has before.
76
Jeremy Austin's throw is in the air . . .

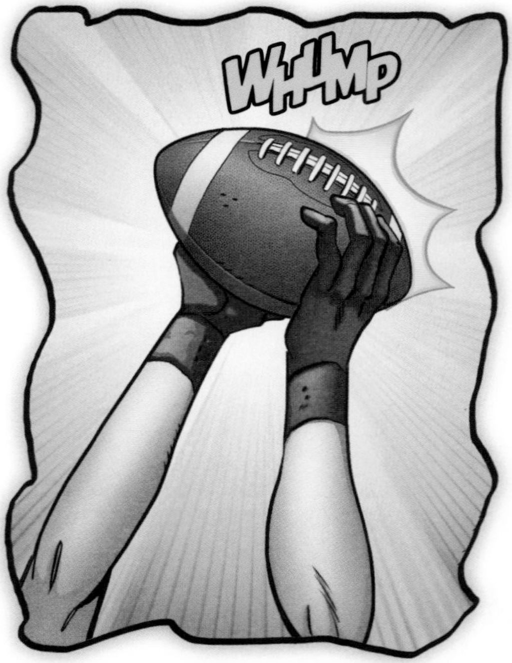
WHUMP

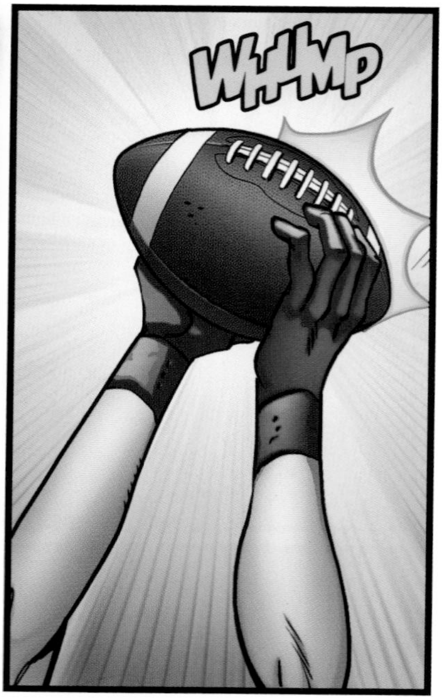
WHUMP

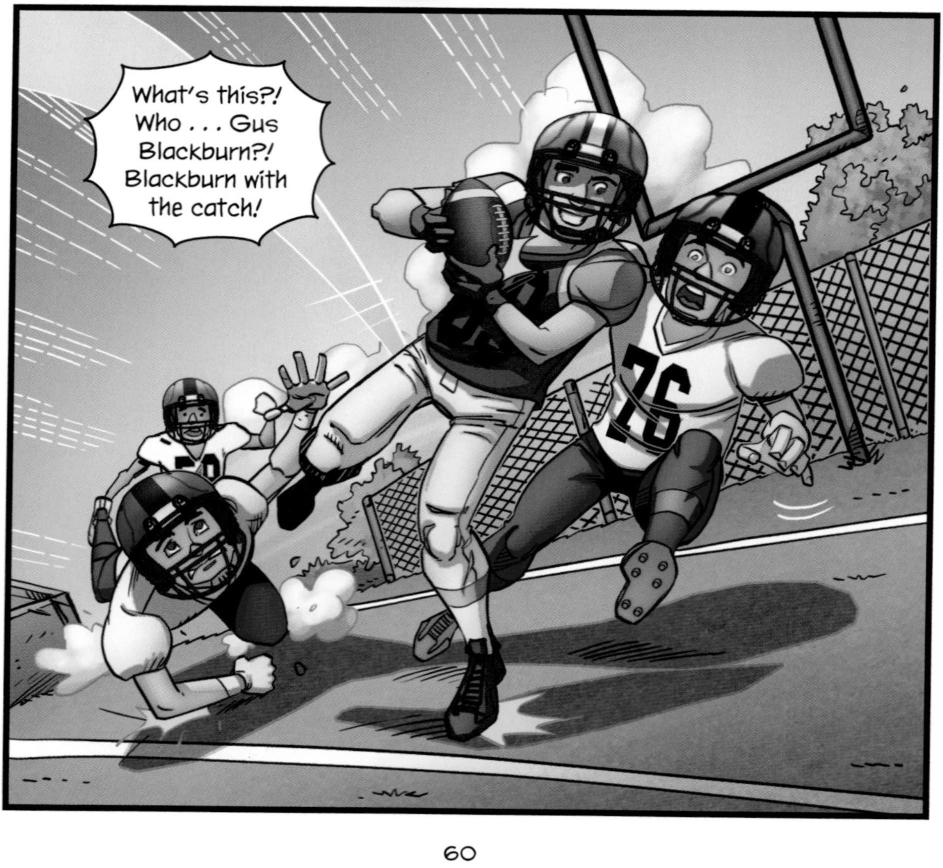
What's this?! Who . . . Gus Blackburn?! Blackburn with the catch!

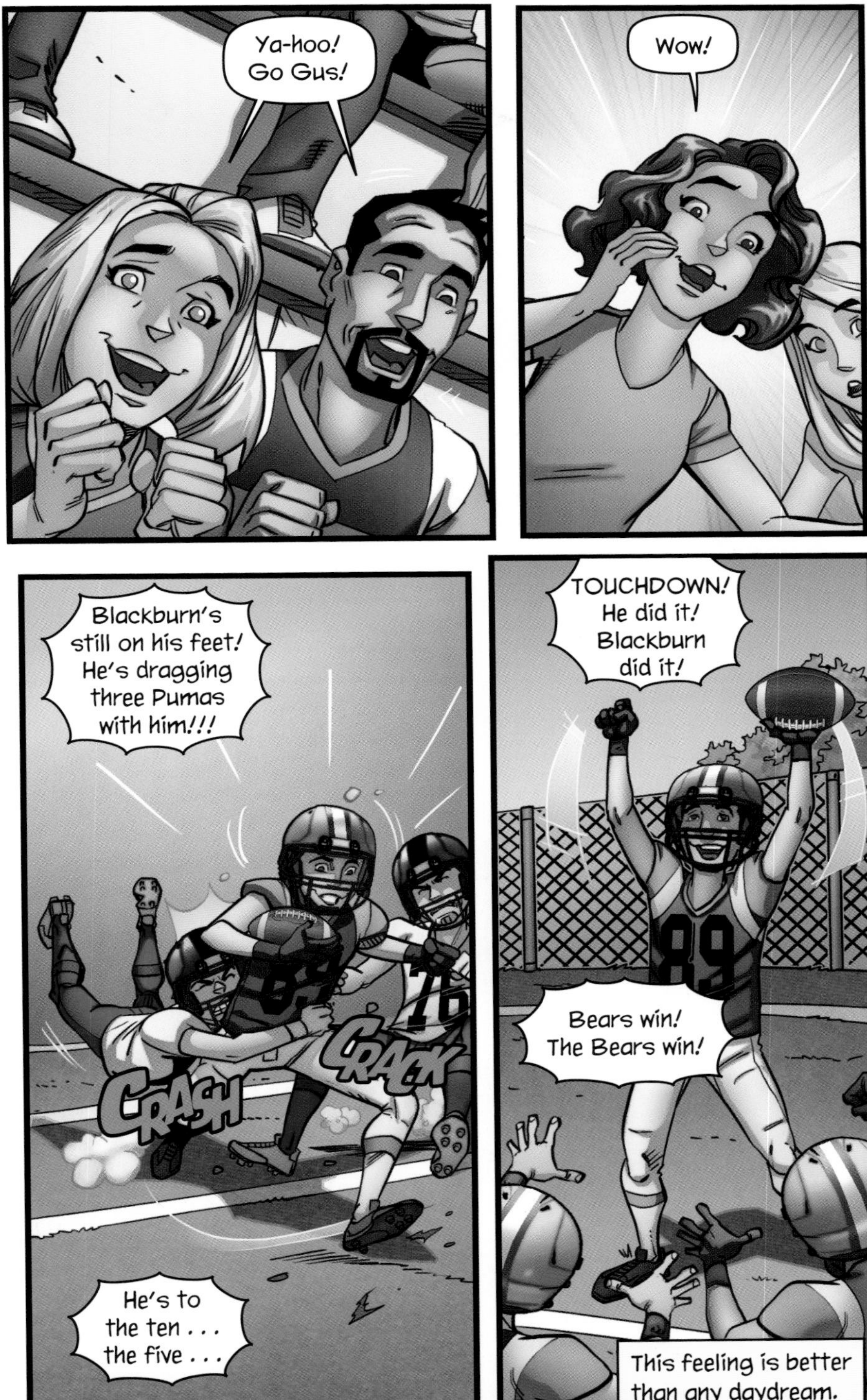
Ya-hoo! Go Gus!
Wow!
Blackburn's still on his feet! He's dragging three Pumas with him!!!
CRASH
CRACK
He's to the ten . . . the five . . .
TOUCHDOWN! He did it! Blackburn did it!
Bears win! The Bears win!
This feeling is better than any daydream.

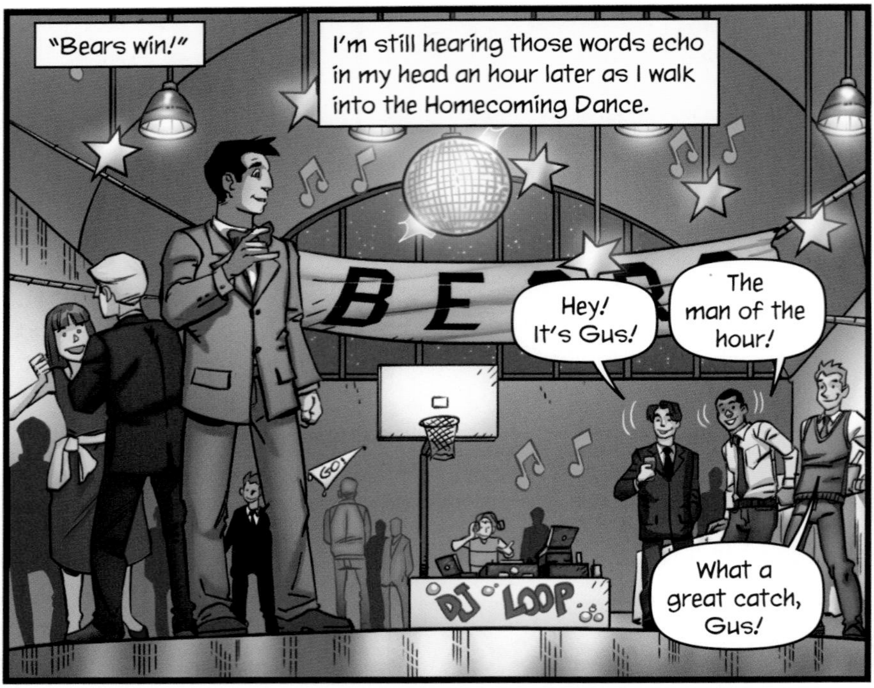
"Bears win!"
I'm still hearing those words echo in my head an hour later as I walk into the Homecoming Dance.
Hey! It's Gus!
The man of the hour!
What a great catch, Gus!
GO!
DJ LOOP

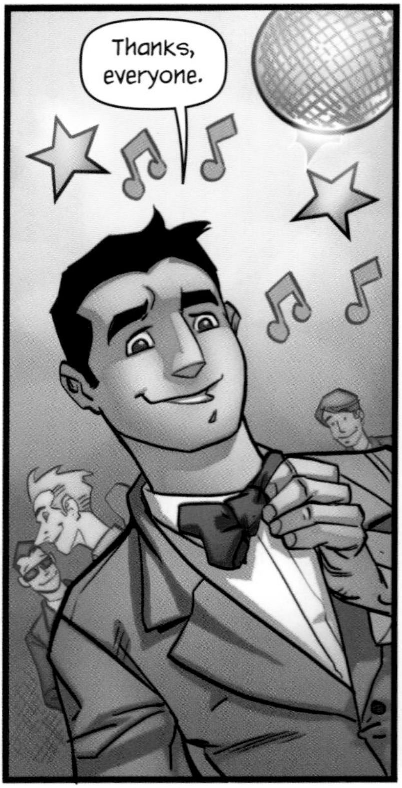
Thanks, everyone.

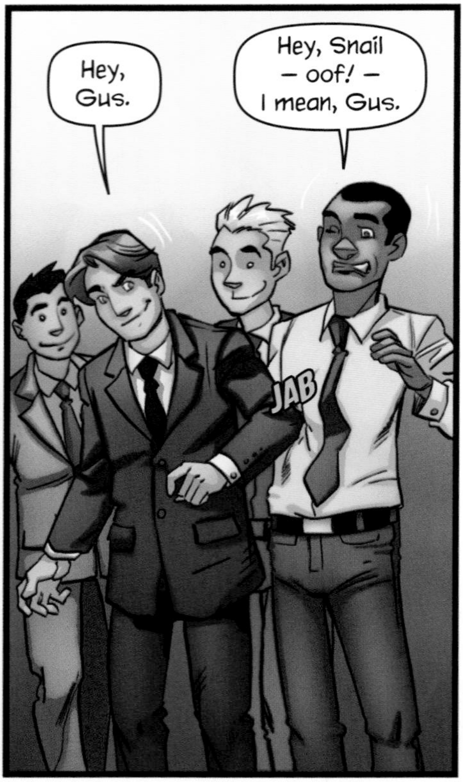
Hey, Gus.
Hey, Snail – oof! – I mean, Gus.
JAB

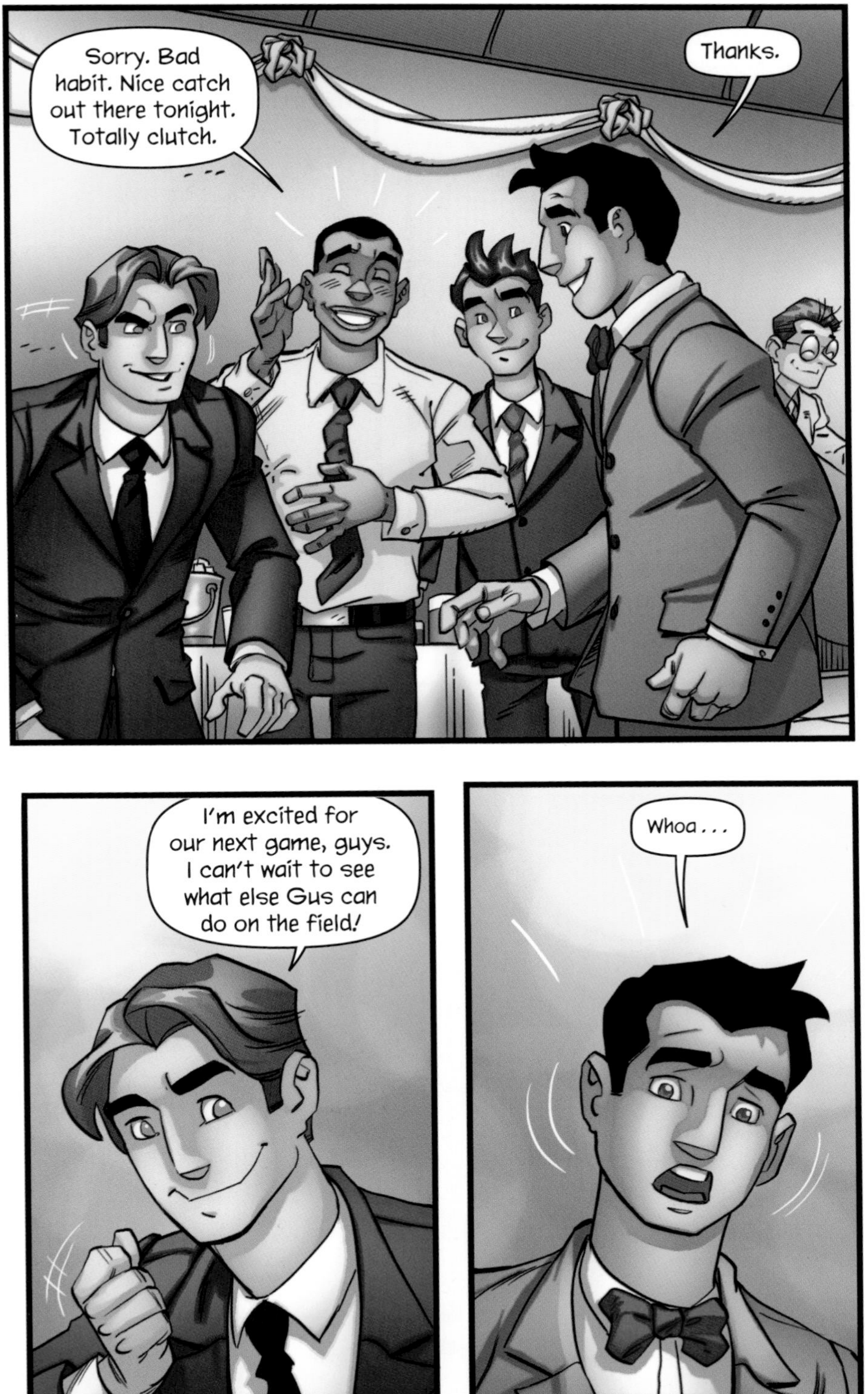
Sorry. Bad habit. Nice catch out there tonight. Totally clutch.
Thanks.
I'm excited for our next game, guys. I can't wait to see what else Gus can do on the field!
Whoa . . .

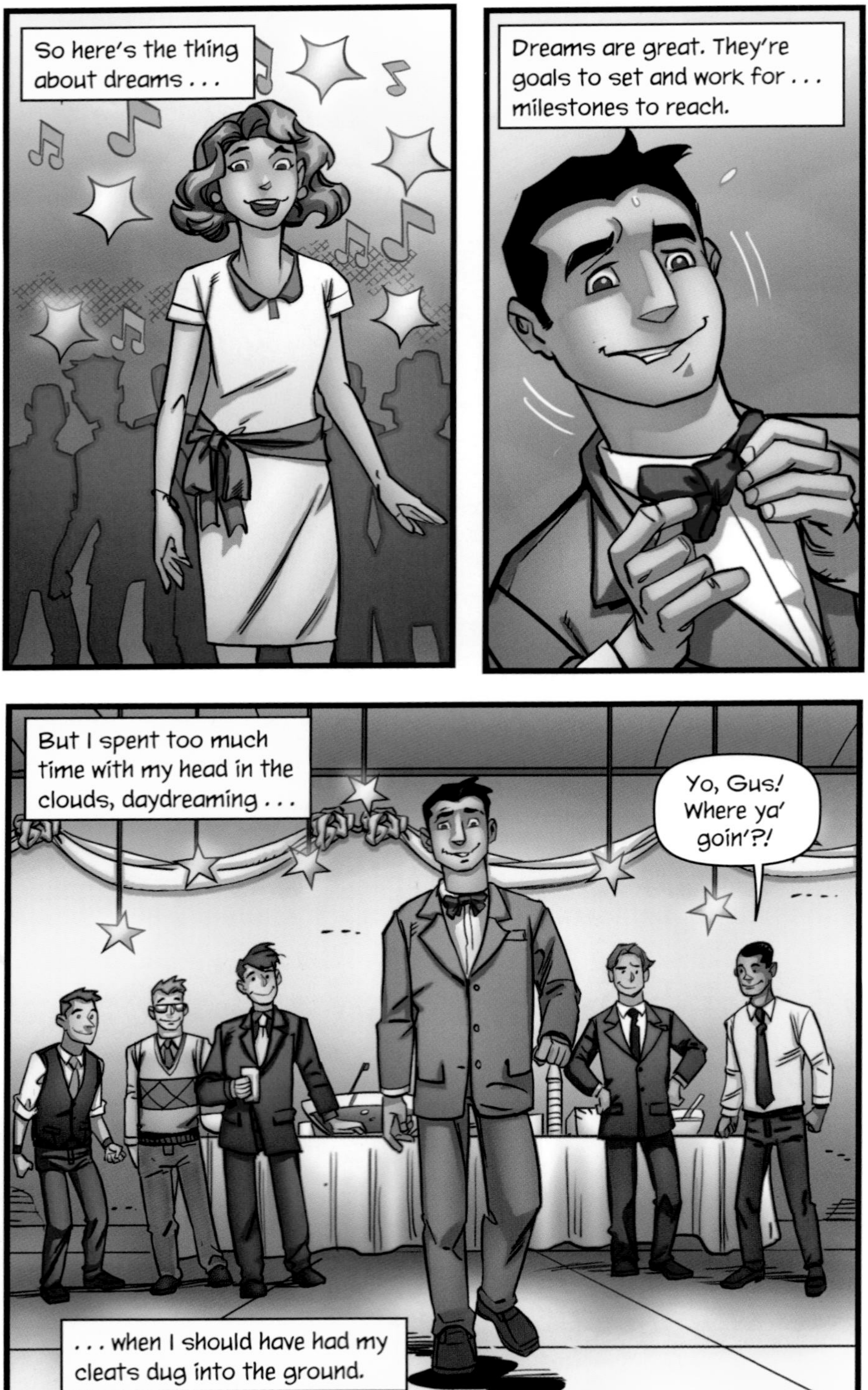
So here's the thing about dreams . . .
Dreams are great. They're goals to set and work for . . . milestones to reach.
But I spent too much time with my head in the clouds, daydreaming . . .
Yo, Gus! Where ya' goin'?!
. . . when I should have had my cleats dug into the ground.

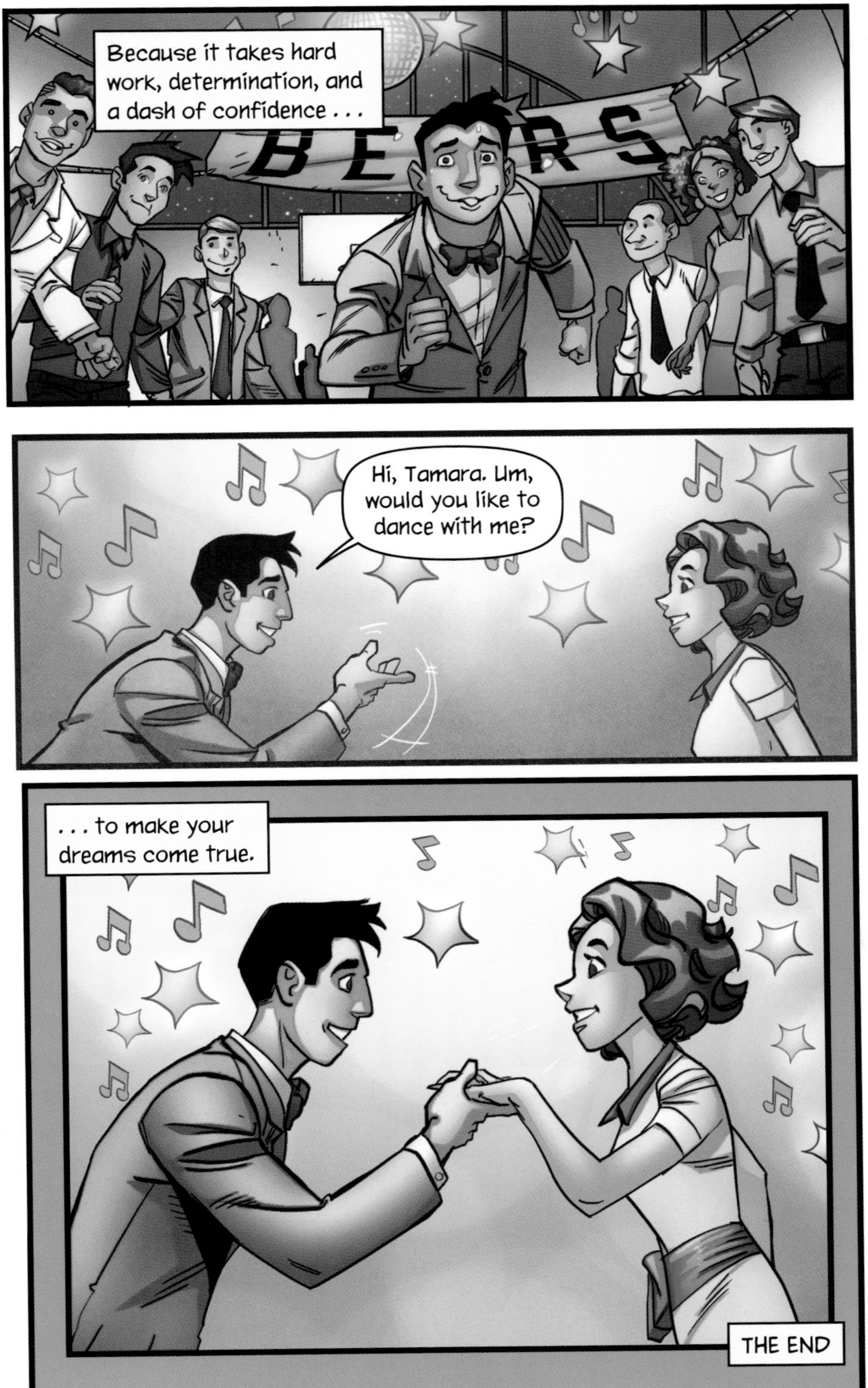
Because it takes hard work, determination, and a dash of confidence . . .
Hi, Tamara. Um, would you like to dance with me?
. . . to make your dreams come true.
THE END

VISUAL QUESTIONS

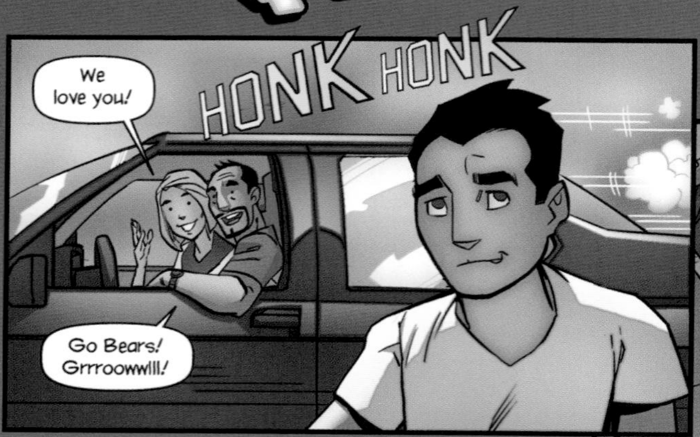

We love you!
HONK HONK
Go Bears! Grrroowwlll!

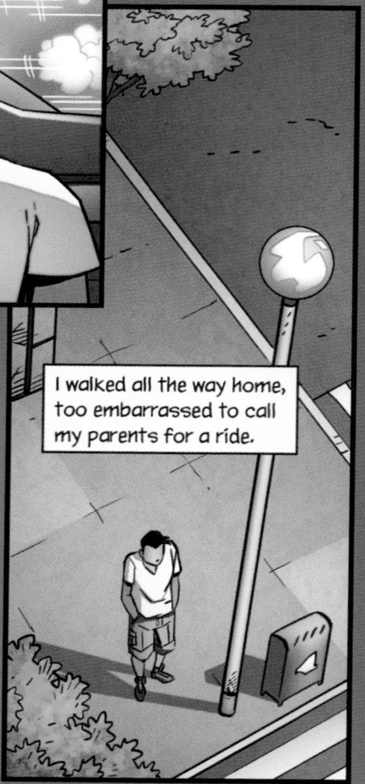

I walked all the way home, too embarrassed to call my parents for a ride.

1. Graphic novels use illustrations to show us how characters are feeling. How do you think Gus feels when his parents honk at him above, or as he stands alone on the street corner? Explain how the art helps to show his feelings in these two scenes.

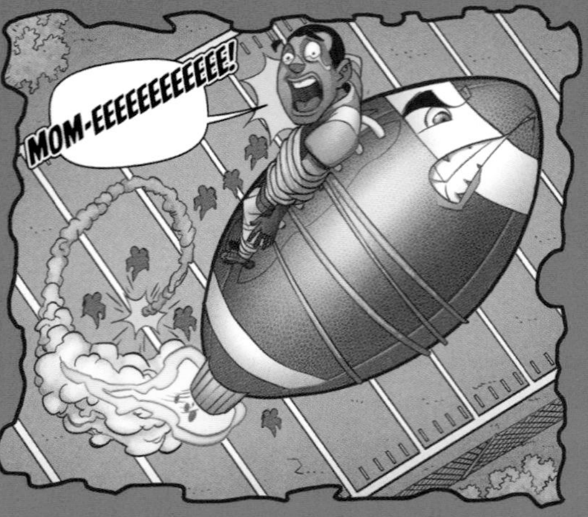

MOM-EEEEEEEEEEEE!

2. Graphic artists use various clues and art styles to tell a story. List the clues the artist used in this panel to show us that this is one of Gus' daydreams?

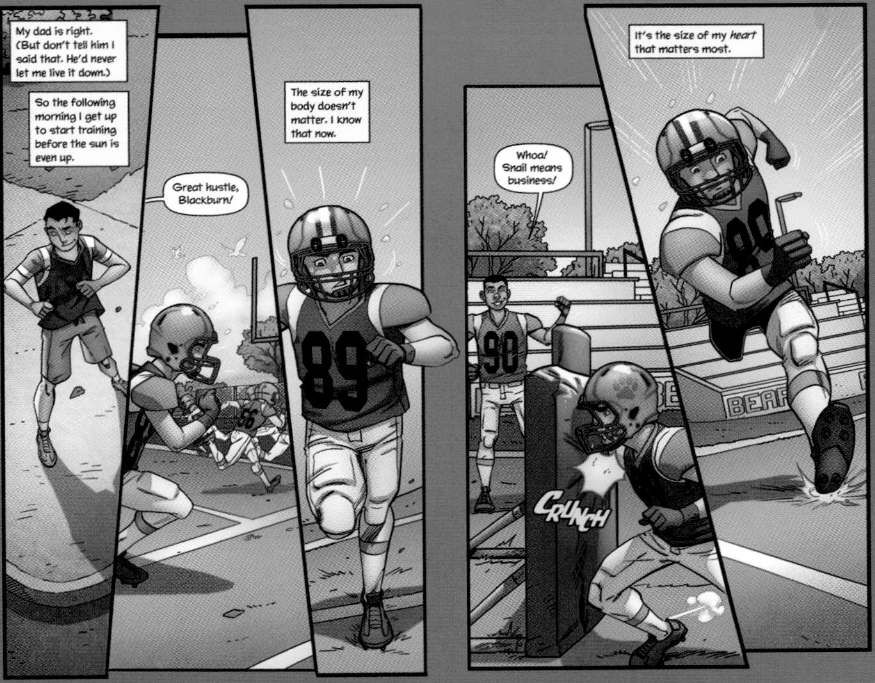
My dad is right. (But don't tell him I said that. He'd never let me live it down.)
So the following morning I get up to start training before the sun is even up.
Great hustle, Blackburn!
The size of my body doesn't matter. I know that now.
Whoa! Snail means business!
CRUNCH
It's the size of my *heart* that matters most.

3. Study the above panels. What actions are being shown? Describe what's happening, and explain how these panels work together to push the story forward.

4. After Gus' heartfelt talk with his dad, he is determined to become the best player he can be. Look at the panel to the right. How does it show us Gus' new attitude and sense of purpose?

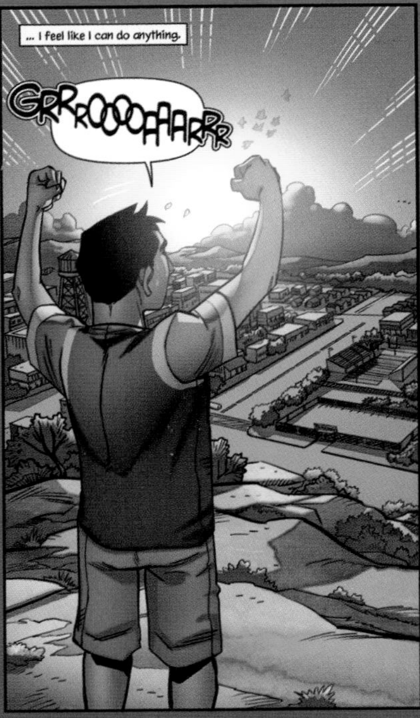
... I feel like I can do anything.
GRRROOOOAAARRR

FOOTBALL POSITIONS

Football teams include both offensive and defensive players. During games, team offenses and defenses each have 11 players on the field at a time.

TEAM DEFENSE

The defense tries to stop the offense from advancing the ball and scoring points. Defensive players tackle opposing runners and try to knock down or catch the offense's passes.

DEFENSIVE TACKLES — the inner two members of the defensive line in charge of stopping running plays

DEFENSIVE ENDS — the outer two members of the defensive line in charge of holding the line of scrimmage

LINEBACKERS — usually the best tacklers on a team who must often defend against running plays as well as passing plays

SAFETIES — these players are the last line of defense and must defend against deep passes and running backs who get by the linebackers

CORNERBACKS — players who line up opposite the offense's wide receivers, they defend deep passes thrown toward the wide parts of the field

TEAM OFFENSE

The offense tries to run and pass the ball downfield to score points and win the game.

QUARTERBACK — the leader of the team who calls plays and yells signals to the team; this player hands the ball to a running back, throws to wide receivers, or runs with the ball

CENTER — the player who snaps the ball to the quarterback

RUNNING BACK — a player who runs with the ball

FULLBACK — a player in charge of blocking for the running back

WIDE RECEIVER — a player who runs downfield, evades defenders, and catches passes from the quarterback

TIGHT END — a player who lines up to the left or right of the quarterback and acts as a receiver and a blocker

LEFT AND RIGHT GUARDS — the inner members of the offensive line who block for the other players

LEFT AND RIGHT TACKLES — the outer two members of the offensive line

GLOSSARY

B-squad (BEE-skwahd)—a group of backup players on a sports team

cleats (KLEETS)—athletic shoes with rubber spikes or wedges on the soles that provide greater traction on grass fields

confidence (KON-fi-duhnss)—to believe in yourself and your own abilities

determination (dih-tur-muh-NAY-shuhn)—to continue trying to achieve a goal no matter how difficult it is

fly-pattern (FLY-PAT-uhrn)—a route run in football in which the wide receiver runs straight upfield toward the end zone

Hail Mary (HAYL MAY-ree)—a play where the quarterback throws the ball deep toward the end zone in the hope that one of the team's receivers will catch it

humiliation (hyoo-mih-lee-AY-shun)—to be made to feel ashamed or foolish by someone else

interception (in-tur-SEP-shun)—a pass caught by a defensive player

milestone (MILE-stone)—an important event or development

playbook (PLAY-book)—a notebook containing descriptions of the plays and strategies used by a sports team

scrimmage (SKRIM-ij)—a practice game

volatile (VOL-uh-tuhl)—unstable or explosive

READ THEM ALL!

JAKE MADDOX
GRAPHIC NOVELS
COMEBACK CATCHER

JAKE MADDOX
GRAPHIC NOVELS
DAYDREAM RECEIVER

JAKE MADDOX
GRAPHIC NOVELS
DOUBLE SCRIBBLE

JAKE MADDOX
GRAPHIC NOVELS
SOCCER SWITCH

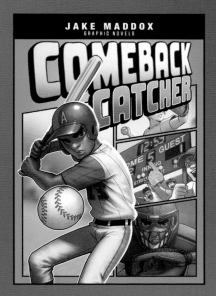

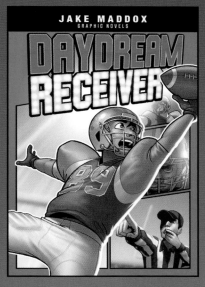

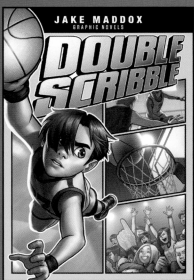

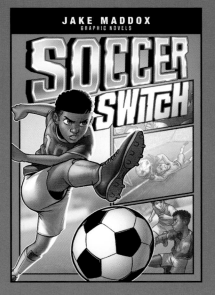

FIND OUT MORE AT
WWW.MYCAPSTONE.COM

BRANDON TERRELL

ABOUT THE AUTHOR

Brandon Terrell is the author of numerous children's books, including several volumes in both the Tony Hawk 900 Revolution series and the Tony Hawk Live2Skate series. He has also written several Spine Shivers titles, and is the author of the Sports Illustrated Kids: Time Machine Magazine series. When not hunched over his laptop, Brandon enjoys watching movies and TV, reading, watching and playing baseball, and spending time with his wife and two children at his home in Minnesota.